Shakespeare on the Double!™

Macbeth

Shakespeare on the Double!™

Macbeth

translated by

Mary Ellen Snodgrass

Wiley Publishing, Inc.

For general information on our other products and services or to obtain technical support please contact our Customer Care Department within the U.S. at (800) 762-2974, outside the U.S. at (317) 572-3993 or fax (317) 572-4002.

Wiley also publishes its books in a variety of electronic formats. Some content that appears in print may not be available in electronic books. For more information about Wiley products, please visit our web site at www.wiley.com.

Library of Congress Cataloging-in-Publication data is available from the publisher upon request.

ISBN-13 978-0-470-04156-7
ISBN-10 0-470-04156-0

Printed in the United States of America

10 9 8 7 6 5 4 3 2 1

Book design by Melissa Auciello-Brogan
Book production by Wiley Publishing, Inc. Composition Services

Contents

ABOUT THE TRANSLATOR

Mary Ellen Snodgrass is an award-winning author of textbooks and general reference works and a former columnist for the *Charlotte Observer.* A member of Phi Beta Kappa, she graduated magna cum laude from the University of North Carolina at Greensboro and Appalachian State University and holds degrees in English, Latin, psychology, and education of gifted children.

Introduction

Shakespeare on the Double! Macbeth provides the full text of the Bard's play side by side with an easy-to-read modern English translation that you can understand. You no longer have to wonder what exactly "Double, double toil and trouble; Fire burn and cauldron bubble" means! You can read the Shakespearean text on the left-hand pages and check the right-hand pages when Shakespeare's language stumps you. Or you can read only the translation, which enables you to understand the action and characters at a more even pace. You can also read both, referring easily between the original text and the modern translation. Any way you choose, you can now fully understand every line of the Bard's masterpiece!

We've also provided you with some additional resources:

- **Brief synopsis** of the plot and action provides a broad-strokes overview of the play.
- **Comprehensive character list** covers the actions, motivations, and characteristics of each major player.
- **Visual character map** displays who the major characters are and how they relate to each other.
- **Cycle of death** pinpoints the sequence of deaths in the play, including who dies, how they die, and why they die.
- **Reflective questions** help you delve even more into the themes and meanings of the play.

Reading Shakespeare can be slow and difficult. No more! With *Shakespeare on the Double! Macbeth,* you can read the play in language that you can grasp quickly and thoroughly.

Synopsis

ACT I

Scene 1

During a storm, a battle sweeps across the Scottish heath. Three hags gather to await a meeting with Macbeth, the Thane of Glamis.

Scene 2

On the battlefield, a captain reports to Duncan, Scotland's king, that the Thane of Cawdor led an insurrection. After Duncan's soldiers put down the rebellion, Duncan condemns the leader to immediate execution. In a battle-field promotion, Duncan plans to elevate Macbeth to Thane of Cawdor.

Scene 3

Macbeth, accompanied by Banquo, his military companion, crosses the plain. Still uninformed of his promotion, Macbeth meets three witches, who predict that he is already Thane of Cawdor and will one day be Scotland's king. The trio prophesy that Banquo will not be king, but he will establish a Scottish dynasty. Angus and Ross report to Macbeth that Duncan has made him Thane of Cawdor. Macbeth muses on the speed with which the first prophecy has come true.

Scene 4

At Duncan's camp, Macbeth invites the king and his court to Inverness castle, the home that Macbeth shares with his wife. Macbeth precedes the royal entourage to alert his staff to make the king feel welcome. Privately, Macbeth ponders an obstacle to ambition—the king's heir, Malcolm, Scotland's crown prince.

Scene 5

Lady Macbeth reads her husband's message concerning his promotion and the witches' prophecy. With letter in hand, she summarizes Macbeth's faults and assumes that he lacks the ambition to seize Scotland's throne. Before Duncan reaches Inverness, she advances from welcoming a royal guest to plotting his murder. When Macbeth arrives, he hesitates to arrange for the king's assassination and leaves the details to Lady Macbeth.

Scene 6
When Duncan surveys Inverness, he praises the pleasant atmosphere. Lady Macbeth offers hospitality due to her king.

Scene 7
In private, Lady Macbeth pushes her husband toward committing regicide. He thinks it wrong to slay the man who has just awarded him a new title. She promises to stand by her husband. At her urging, he agrees to kill Duncan.

ACT II

Scene 1
Banquo and Macbeth have contrasting responses to the witches' predictions. Banquo is too honest to behave dishonorably. When Macbeth is alone, he visualizes a dagger floating in the air with its handle toward his hand. The blade drips blood.

Scene 2
After Lady Macbeth places a sedative in the wine cups of Duncan's bodyguard and strikes the signal bell, Macbeth slips by the sleepers and stabs the king. On the way down the hall, Macbeth hears a guest asking for God's blessing. Because Macbeth can't reply "amen," he is shocked at his culpability. Trembling, he goes back to his room. Lady Macbeth scolds him for removing the swords from the crime scene. She returns them to Duncan's grooms, then returns to her room to have Macbeth wash away the blood and go to bed.

Scene 3
The doorkeeper is still drunk from the night's celebration when someone knocks at the castle gate. He opens the door to Lenox and Macduff. Macbeth joins them. Macduff goes to Duncan's room and returns shaken by the sight of the king's slaughtered corpse. As report of the murder spreads, Macbeth summons Lady Macbeth and the king's sons, Malcolm and Donalbain. As though in anger, Macbeth kills the startled grooms.

Lady Macbeth pretends to faint. In the turmoil, the two princes realize that they must escape before the investigation charges them with Duncan's death or before the murderer makes them the next victims.

Scene 4

Outside Inverness castle, Ross and an elderly man consider how much uproar has resulted from Duncan's murder. Macduff announces that Donaldbain and Malcolm face accusations of killing the king. Macduff also reports that Macbeth succeeds Duncan on Scotland's throne. Ross leaves immediately for Macbeth's crowning at Scone, the traditional site of Scotland's coronations. Macduff remains behind at Fife.

3

ACT III

Scene 1

Banquo suspects that Macbeth has killed Duncan. On the evening of a state dinner, Macbeth learns that Banquo and his son Fleance are going out on horseback before returning to the banquet. Lest Banquo produce a dynasty as the witches prophesied, Macbeth sends two assassins to murder Banquo and Fleance. The king manipulates the killers by blaming Banquo for all Scotland's problems.

Scene 2

Macbeth joins Lady Macbeth in assessing their political situation. She fears that her husband reveals his criminality by looking guilty.

Scene 3

At nightfall, a third murderer joins the two assassins. After they ambush and murder Banquo in a ditch, Fleance rides off.

Scene 4

The chief assassin returns during the banquet to inform Macbeth that they successfully killed Banquo, but not Fleance. Macbeth returns to the formalities and envisions Banquo's ghost sitting in the king's chair. As guests mutter at their host's bizarre illusion, Lady Macbeth reports that the king has long been troubled by hallucinations. A second outburst ends the state banquet. Lady Macbeth excuses all from the hall. Macbeth longs to hear more prophecy from the witches. She encourages him to sleep.

Scene 5

Hecate, the head witch, chides the three hags for toying with Macbeth without her advice. She instructs them in stirring up a spell for Macbeth.

Scene 6

Meanwhile, Lenox and another noble debate the cause of Duncan's and Banquo's murders and the reason why Malcolm fled to England. Because Macduff has joined Malcolm at the court of King Edward, Lenox surmises that the English will lead a revolt in Scotland to restore rule to Duncan's heir.

ACT IV

Scene 1

Hecate and the three hags continue boiling ingredients in their pot. Macbeth arrives to demand a more detailed view of the future. The three witches summon a series of illusions. First comes an armored head to alert Macbeth to danger from Macduff. A second illusion consists of a bloody child, who declares that Macbeth can never suffer harm from enemies born normally of woman. The last illusion, a child wearing a crown, signifies that Macbeth will be undefeated until Birnam wood marches on Dunsinane hill. The three illusions elate Macbeth. He deduces that his reign will be unchallenged.

Still hungry for glimpses of the future, Macbeth demands that the witches tell him about danger from Fleance. A fourth illusion is a procession of eight kings following Banquo's ghost. At the end of the vision, the magic cauldron sinks and the witches vanish. A messenger reports that Macduff has fled Scotland. Because of the first illusion, Macbeth begins plotting the slaying of Macduff's family.

Scene 2

Lady Macduff charges her husband with abandoning her and leaving her children vulnerable to attack. After a brief warning of danger, she encounters murderers, who slaughter Macduff's son along with Lady Macduff and her other children and servants.

Scene 3

Meanwhile, Malcolm confers with Macduff at the court of King Edward in England. Through trickery, Malcolm elicits proof of his patriotism. Ross reports that rebellion is growing in Scotland. Under duress, he adds details of Macbeth's raid on Fife and the slaying of Lady Macduff, her children, and the servants. Macduff transforms his rage into military might. He joins Malcolm and Siward the Elder in leading a rebellion against Scotland's tyrant king.

ACT V

Scene 1

At Dunsinane castle, a doctor and a lady-in-waiting discuss and observe Lady Macbeth's mental aberrations. Carrying a candle, she sleepwalks, writes notes, and tries to wash imaginary blood from her hand. From her babblings, the doctor and lady deduce that Lady Macbeth joined Macbeth in murdering the king and in spreading terror over Scotland. The observers wisely keep quiet about their conclusions.

Scene 2

Outside Dunsinane castle, Malcolm, Macduff, and Siward the Elder lead ten thousand English troops to Birnam wood.

Scene 3

Macbeth clings to the prophecies that imply that he is safe from harm. The physician reports that Lady Macbeth suffers mental illness. Macbeth declares that he has no faith in medicine.

Scene 4

Malcolm orders the troops to chop down branches and to camouflage their approach by walking behind the leaves. He intends to conceal from Macbeth the size of the rebel force.

Scene 5

After investigating a cry from the women's quarters, Seyton informs Macbeth that Lady Macbeth is dead. Macbeth is not surprised that her condition worsened to her demise. He believes that life is useless.

Scene 6

Malcolm commands the troops to drop the tree limbs and attack Dunsinane castle.

Scene 7

A trembling, white-faced servant reports that Birnam wood appears to move toward Dunsinane. Macbeth's courage crumbles after he realizes that the witches predicted the revolt. He slays Siward the Younger in a duel and hurries on to confront Macduff.

Scene 8

Rejecting suicide, Macbeth clings to the hope that no man born of woman will threaten him. Macduff, too enraged for words, shatters all false hopes by revealing that he was surgically removed from his mother's womb. Knowing that he is guilty of murdering Lady Macduff and her family, Macbeth stoically clashes with Macduff. Macduff returns to Malcolm with Macbeth's severed head and proclaims Malcolm Scotland's rightful king. In reward to his supporters, Malcolm proclaims them Scotland's first earls.

List of Characters

Macbeth   The Thane (Lord) of Glamis and a leader in Duncan's army, later the Thane of Cawdor. When three witches predict that he will one day be King of Scotland, he allows his ambition and that of his wife to over-come his loyalty to King Duncan, who is Macbeth's kinsman. Macbeth's bloody reign culminates in a battle against Malcolm and the English forces.

Lady Macbeth   The scheming wife of Macbeth, whose ambition helps to drive her husband toward murdering Scotland's king. Subsequently, her husband's cruelty and her own guilt drive her to sleepwalking and madness.

Banquo   A fellow soldier and companion of Macbeth, who also receives a prophecy from the three witches that his children will one day succeed to the throne of Scotland. This information causes Macbeth to hire killers to ambush and assassinate Banquo. At a state dinner, Banquo's ghost ter-rifies Macbeth.

Duncan   King of Scotland. His victories against rebellious kinsmen and the Norwegians bring him honor and the love of Scots. His decision to pass the kingdom to his son Malcolm provokes Duncan's untimely stabbing at the hands of Macbeth, Duncan's kinsman.

Fleance   Banquo's son, who, by escaping Macbeth's plot on his life, is fated to father a line of kings.

Donalbain and Malcolm   Duncan's two sons. Fearful of implication in their father's murder, they flee Scotland, Donalbain to Ireland and Malcolm who is heir to the throne to England. With the aid of King Edward of England, Malcolm raises a landing force to unseat the tyrant Macbeth.

Macduff   A thane (lord) of Scotland who discovers the murdered King Duncan. Suspecting Macbeth and eventually turning against him, Macduff later flees to England to join Malcolm. After Macbeth masterminds the murder of Lady Macbeth and her children, Macduff faces Macbeth in a duel and avenges the loss of the Macduff household.

Lady Macduff and her son   Innocent victims of Macbeth's assassins. Lady Macduff, in the absence of her husband, is unable to ward off the murderers who slay the entire household.

Lennox, Ross, Menteith, Angus, Caithness   Scots nobles who turn against the tyrannical Macbeth.

The Porter, the Old Man, the Doctor   Three commentators on events, all of whom have a certain degree of wisdom and foresight. The Porter hints at the hellish nature of Macbeth's castle; the Old Man associates the murder of King Duncan with the instability of the natural world; the Doctor recognizes mental unrest in Lady Macbeth, whose madness is incurable.

Hecate and the Witches   Three agents of Fate who reveal the future to Macbeth and Banquo and who later appear to confirm the downfall and tragic destiny of the tyrannical Macbeth. Leading the unnamed three witches is Hecate.

Character Map

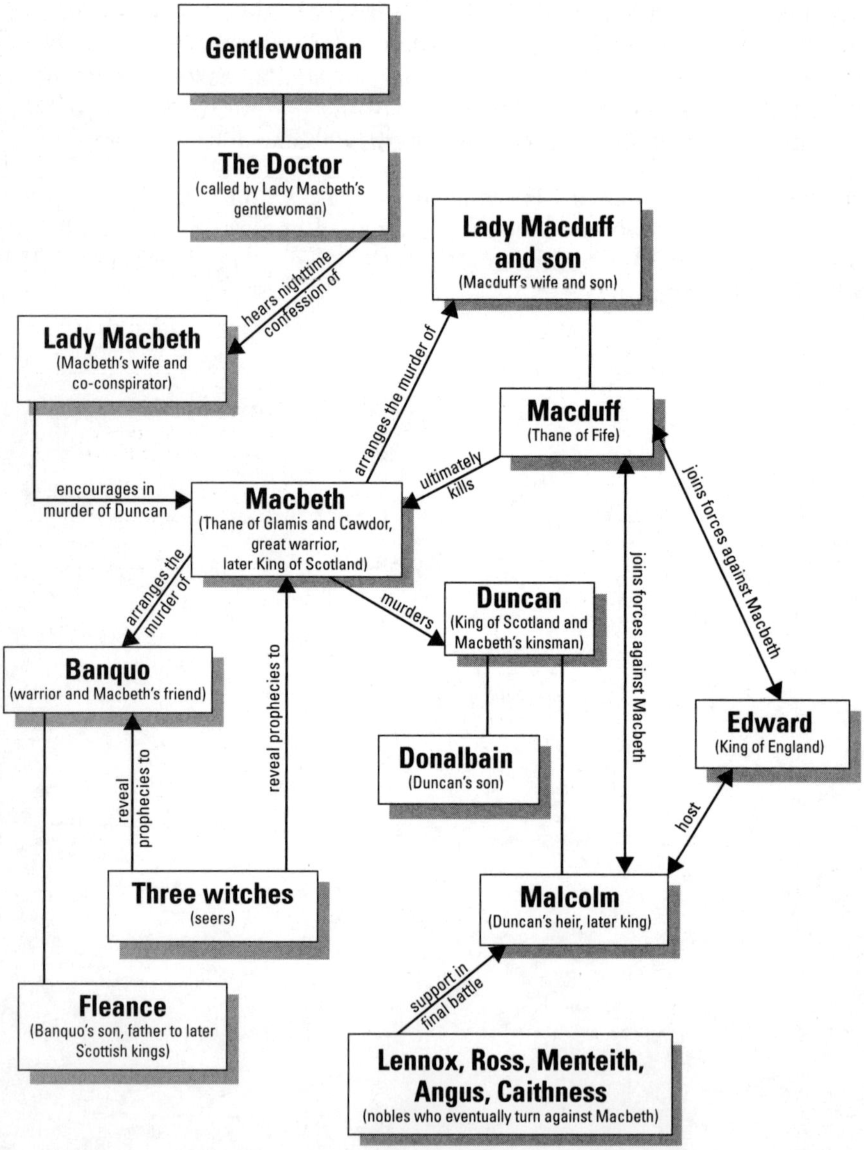

Cycle of Death

"Vaulting ambition" is the motivation for multiple murders in Macbeth. Goaded by his wife, Macbeth hurries prophecies of greatness by murdering the King of Scotland. From this point on, the tragedy spirals downward with ambush, swordplay, suicide, and the execution of a mother and her children. The graphic below outlines the sequence of deaths.

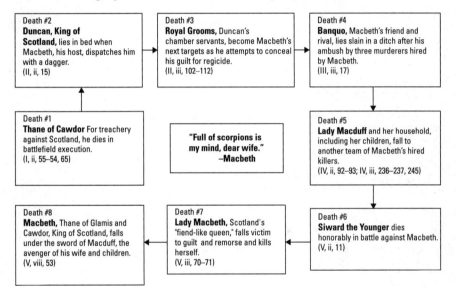

Death #2
Duncan, King of Scotland, lies in bed when Macbeth, his host, dispatches him with a dagger.
(II, ii, 15)

Death #3
Royal Grooms, Duncan's chamber servants, become Macbeth's next targets as he attempts to conceal his guilt for regicide.
(II, iii, 102–112)

Death #4
Banquo, Macbeth's friend and rival, lies slain in a ditch after his ambush by three murderers hired by Macbeth.
(III, iii, 17)

Death #1
Thane of Cawdor For treachery against Scotland, he dies in battlefield execution.
(I, ii, 55–54, 65)

"Full of scorpions is my mind, dear wife."
—Macbeth

Death #5
Lady Macduff and her household, including her children, fall to another team of Macbeth's hired killers.
(IV, ii, 92–93; IV, iii, 236–237, 245)

Death #8
Macbeth, Thane of Glamis and Cawdor, King of Scotland, falls under the sword of Macduff, the avenger of his wife and children.
(V, viii, 53)

Death #7
Lady Macbeth, Scotland's "fiend-like queen," falls victim to guilt and remorse and kills herself.
(V, iii, 70–71)

Death #6
Siward the Younger dies honorably in battle against Macbeth.
(V, ii, 11)

Shakespeare's
Macbeth

ACT I, SCENE 1

A desert heath.

[Thunder and lightning. Enter three Witches]

FIRST WITCH	When shall we three meet again In thunder, lightning, or in rain?
SECOND WITCH	When the Hurlyburly's done, When the battle's lost and won.
THIRD WITCH	That will be ere the set of sun.
FIRST WITCH	Where the place?
SECOND WITCH	Upon the heath.
THIRD WITCH	There to meet with Macbeth.
FIRST WITCH	I come, Graymalkin!
SECOND WITCH	Paddock calls.
THIRD WITCH	Anon.
ALL	Fair is foul, and foul is fair: Hover through the fog and filthy air. *[Exeunt]*

5

10

ACT I, SCENE 1

A deserted plain.

[Thunder and lightning. Enter three Witches]

FIRST WITCH   When should we next gather, in a thunderstorm or just rain?

SECOND WITCH   When the uproar is over, when the battle ends.

THIRD WITCH   It will end before sunset.

FIRST WITCH   Where shall we meet?

SECOND WITCH   On the plain.

THIRD WITCH   To meet Macbeth.

FIRST WITCH   I'm coming, my gray kitty!

SECOND WITCH   My toad is waiting.

THIRD WITCH   Hurry.

ALL   Good is evil, and evil is good: linger in the fog and war-corrupted air. *[They depart]*

ACT I, SCENE 2

A camp near Forres.

[Alarum within. Enter KING DUNCAN, MALCOLM, DONALBAIN, LENNOX with Attendants, meeting a bleeding Sergeant]

DUNCAN   What bloody man is that? He can report,
As seemeth by his plight, of the revolt
The newest state.

MALCOLM   This is the sergeant
Who, like a good and hardy soldier, fought
'Gainst my captivity. Hail, brave friend!   5
Say to the king the knowledge of the broil
As thou didst leave it.

SERGEANT   Doubtful it stood;
As two spent swimmers, that do cling together
And choke their art. The merciless Macdonwald—
Worthy to be a rebel, for to that   10
The multiplying villanies of nature
Do swarm upon him—from the western isles
Of kerns and gallowglasses is supplied;
And fortune, on his damned quarrel smiling,
Show'd like a rebel's whore: but all's too weak;   15
For brave Macbeth,—well he deserves that name,—
Disdaining fortune, with his brandish'd steel,
Which smok'd with bloody execution,
Like valour's minion carv'd out his passage
Till he fac'd the slave;   20
Which ne'er shook hands, nor bade farewell to him,
Till he unseam'd him from the nave to the chaps,
And fix'd his head upon our battlements.

DUNCAN   O valiant cousin! worthy gentleman!

SERGEANT   As whence the sun 'gins his reflection   25
Shipwracking storms and direful thunders break,
So from that spring whence comfort seem'd to come
Discomfort swells. Mark, King of Scotland, mark:
No sooner justice had with valour arm'd
Compell'd these skipping kerns to trust their heels,   30
But the Norweyan lord, surveying vantage,
With furbish'd arms and new supplies of men
Began a fresh assault.

ORIGINAL

ACT I, SCENE 2

A camp near Forres, an ancient capital city in northern Scotland on the Moray coast.

ACT I

[A call to arms in the camp. Enter KING DUNCAN, MALCOLM, DONALBAIN, LENNOX with Attendants, meeting a bleeding Sergeant]

DUNCAN Who is that wounded man? He might know the situation on the battlefield.

MALCOLM This is the loyal, valiant sergeant who saved me from capture. Welcome, brave soldier! Report to King Duncan the status of the battle when you left the field.

SERGEANT It was nip and tuck, like two tired swimmers hanging on to each other and pulling each other under water. The vengeful Macdonwald—a born rebel blessed with treachery—brings light and heavy-armed infantry from the Hebrides islands off Scotland's west coast. And luck favors him like a smiling prostitute, but luck is not enough. Against Macdonwald, brave Macbeth—deserving our praise—ignored luck. Raising his sword, which dripped blood, he made a path through the battle until he reached Macdonwald. Macbeth said nothing to the rebel, but split him from gut to jaws and perched his head on the camp wall.

DUNCAN A brave kinsman! A deserving gentleman!

SERGEANT Just as thunderstorms arise in the east, bad news comes from the same direction. Note, Duncan, that as soon as our army put down the revolt and sent the rebels running, the king of Norway took advantage of our weary soldiers by sending his forces against us.

DUNCAN   Dismay'd not this
                 Our captains, Macbeth and Banquo?

SERGEANT   Yes;
                 As sparrows eagles, or the hare the lion.   35
                 If I say sooth, I must report they were
                 As cannons overcharg'd with double cracks;
                 So they doubly redoubled strokes upon the foe:
                 Except they meant to bathe in reeking wounds,
                 Or memorize another Golgotha,   40
                 I cannot tell—
                 But I am faint, my gashes cry for help.

DUNCAN   So well thy words become thee as thy wounds;
                 They smack of honour both. Go, get him surgeons.
                 [Exeunt SERGEANT, attended]
                 [Enter ROSS]
                 Who comes here?   45

MALCOLM   The worthy Thane of Ross.

LENNOX   What a haste looks through his eyes! So should he look
                 That seems to speak things strange.

ROSS   God save the king!

DUNCAN   Whence cam'st thou, worthy thane?

ROSS   From Fife, great king;
                 Where the Norweyan banners flout the sky   50
                 And fan our people cold. Norway himself.
                 With terrible numbers,
                 Assisted by that most disloyal traitor,
                 The Thane of Cawdor, began a dismal conflict;
                 Till that Bellona's bridegroom, lapp'd in proof,   55
                 Confronted him with self-comparisons,
                 Point against point, rebellious arm 'gainst arm,
                 Curbing his lavish spirit: and, to conclude,
                 The victory fell on us.—

DUNCAN   Great happiness!

DUNCAN	Did this new assault trouble our leaders, Macbeth and Banquo?
SERGEANT	No more than a sparrow threatens an eagle or a hare frightens a lion. I can truly report that they fought like cannons loaded with a double charge. Macbeth and Banquo fought twice as hard, as though they were bathing in blood or reenacting Christ's crucifixion. I can't say more—I am weak from loss of blood. My wounds need tending.
DUNCAN	Your report and battle wounds attest to your loyal service. You deserve honor. Call the medics to treat this man. *[The sergeant and aides depart]* *[Enter ROSS]* Who are you?
MALCOLM	He is Lord Ross.
LENNOX	Look at his eyes! He is eager to tell you something.
ROSS	God save the king!
DUNCAN	Where did you come from, Lord Ross?
ROSS	From Fife on Scotland's southeastern coast, sire, where Norwegian soldiers wave their banners over the fearful Scots. The king of Norway, leading a large force, launched battle against us with the aid of Lord Cawdor, a wretched traitor. Macbeth, still in armor, faced him man to man and halted his bold advance. In the end, our soldiers won.
DUNCAN	What good news!

ROSS   That now
              Sweno, the Norways' king, craves composition;   60
              Nor would we deign him burial of his men
              Till he disbursed, at Saint Colme's Inch,
              Ten thousand dollars to our general use.

DUNCAN   No more that Thane of Cawdor shall deceive
              Our bosom interest. Go pronounce his present death,   65
              And with his former title greet Macbeth.

ROSS   I'll see it done.

DUNCAN   What he hath lost noble Macbeth hath won. *[Exeunt]*

ROSS	Sweno, the king of Norway, asks for terms of surrender. We refused to let him bury his dead until he deposited $10,000 at the island of Saint Columba.
DUNCAN	Lord Cawdor shall never deceive us again. Condemn him to death and confer his title on Macbeth.
ROSS	I will.
DUNCAN	What Lord Cawdor forfeited belongs to Macbeth. *[They depart]*

ACT I, SCENE 3

A heath.

[Thunder. Enter the three Witches]

FIRST WITCH	Where hast thou been, sister?
SECOND WITCH	Killing swine.
THIRD WITCH	Sister, where thou?

FIRST WITCH A sailor's wife had chestnuts in her lap,
And munch'd, and munch'd, and munch'd: 'Give
    me,' quoth I: 5
'Aroint thee, witch!' the rump-fed ronyon cries.
Her husband's to Aleppo gone, master o' the Tiger:
But in a sieve I'll thither sail,
And, like a rat without a tail,
I'll do, I'll do, and I'll do.   10

SECOND WITCH I'll give thee a wind.

FIRST WITCH Thou'rt kind.

THIRD WITCH And I another.

FIRST WITCH I myself have all the other;
And the very ports they blow,   15
All the quarters that they know
I' the shipman's card.
I'll drain him dry as hay:
Sleep shall neither night nor day
Hang upon his pent-house lid;   20
He shall live a man forbid.
Weary se'nnights nine times nine
Shall he dwindle, peak and pine:
Though his bark cannot be lost,
Yet it shall be tempest-tost.   25
Look what I have.

SECOND WITCH Show me, show me.

FIRST WITCH Here I have a pilot's thumb,
Wrack'd as homeward he did come. *[Drum within]*

THIRD WITCH A drum! a drum!   30
Macbeth doth come.

ACT I, SCENE 3

A plain.

[Thunder. Enter the three Witches]

FIRST WITCH   Where were you, sister?

SECOND WITCH   Killing pigs.

THIRD WITCH   Sister, where were you?

FIRST WITCH   The wife of a sailor was munching chestnuts. I asked for one. The fat cow yelled, "Off with you, witch!" Her husband sails on the *Tiger* to Aleppo off the coast of Syria. I'll follow him in a sieve and, like a tailless rat, I'll hex his ship.

SECOND WITCH   I'll supply wind.

FIRST WITCH   You are kind.

THIRD WITCH   And I will supply more wind.

FIRST WITCH   I have more wind to blow each port on every point of the compass. I'll dry him out like hay. He won't sleep a wink. He will feel like a doomed man. For seven days he will weaken. Although his ship won't sink, it will be tumbled on high seas. Look what I have.

SECOND WITCH   Show me, show me.

FIRST WITCH   I have the thumb of a ship's pilot who lost it during a hard voyage home. *[A military drum sounds in the camp]*

THIRD WITCH   According to the drum taps, Macbeth is approaching.

ALL	The weird sisters, hand in hand,
	Posters of the sea and land,
	Thus do go about, about:
	Thrice to thine, and thrice to mine, 35
	And thrice again, to make up nine.
	Peace! the charm's wound up.
	[Enter MACBETH and BANQUO]
MACBETH	So foul and fair a day I have not seen.
BANQUO	How far is 't call'd to Forres? What are these,
	So wither'd and so wild in their attire, 40
	That look not like th' inhabitants o' the earth,
	And yet are on 't? Live you? or are you aught
	That man may question? You seem to understand me,
	By each at once her choppy finger laying
	Upon her skinny lips: you should be women, 45
	And yet your beards forbid me to interpret
	That you are so.
MACBETH	Speak, if you can: what are you?
FIRST WITCH	All hail, Macbeth! hail to thee, Thane of Glamis!
SECOND WITCH	All hail, Macbeth! hail to thee, Thane of Cawdor!
THIRD WITCH	All hail, Macbeth! that shalt be king hereafter. 50
BANQUO	Good Sir, why do you start, and seem to fear
	Things that do sound so fair? I' the name of truth,
	Are ye fantastical, or that indeed
	Which outwardly ye show? My noble partner 55
	You greet with present grace and great prediction
	Of noble having and of royal hope,
	That he seems rapt withal: to me you speak not.
	If you can look into the seeds of time,
	And say which grain will grow and which will not, 60
	Speak then to me, who neither beg nor fear
	Your favours nor your hate.
FIRST WITCH	Hail!
SECOND WITCH	Hail!
THIRD WITCH	Hail! 65
FIRST WITCH	Lesser than Macbeth, and greater.

ORIGINAL

ALL	The witches, who travel sea and land, join hands and rotate in a circle. To cast a spell, they circle three times in one direction, three times in the reverse direction, and three times in the original direction to make up the magic number nine. Quiet, the circle has cast a powerful charm. *[Enter MACBETH and BANQUO]*
MACBETH	I have never seen so dreadful and wonderful a day.
BANQUO	Who are these wild, dried-up creatures? They stand on earth, but don't look like earthlings. Are you alive? Can I question you? You seem to understand me because you place chapped fingers on your lips. You look like females, but women don't have beards like yours.
MACBETH	Tell us, what are you?
FIRST WITCH	We honor you, Macbeth, Lord of Glamis!
SECOND WITCH	We honor you, Macbeth, Lord of Cawdor!
THIRD WITCH	We honor you, Macbeth, a future king.
BANQUO	Sir, why do you flinch from for so wonderful a prediction? Are you women fantasies or are you truly females? My lordly comrade, you seem amazed to be greeted as a future king, but you say nothing. If you witches know the future, tell me. I want nothing from you. I'm not afraid of your powers.
FIRST WITCH	Welcome!
SECOND WITCH	Welcome!
THIRD WITCH	Welcome!
FIRST WITCH	You are less noble than Macbeth, but you will be greater.

SECOND WITCH   Not so happy, yet much happier.

THIRD WITCH   Thou shalt get kings, though thou be none:
So, all hail, Macbeth and Banquo!

FIRST WITCH   Banquo and Macbeth, all hail!   70

MACBETH   Stay, you imperfect speakers, tell me more:
By Sinel's death I know I am Thane of Glamis;
But how of Cawdor? the Thane of Cawdor lives,
A prosperous gentleman; and to be king
Stands not within the prospect of belief,   75
No more than to be Cawdor. Say from whence
You owe this strange intelligence? or why
Upon this blasted heath you stop our way
With such prophetic greeting? Speak, I charge you.
[Witches vanish]

BANQUO   The earth hath bubbles as the water has,   80
And these are of them. Whither are they vanish'd?

MACBETH   Into the air, and what seem'd corporal melted
As breath into the wind. Would they had stay'd!

BANQUO   Were such things here as we do speak about?
Or have we eaten on the insane root   85
That takes the reason prisoner?

MACBETH   Your children shall be kings.

BANQUO   You shall be king.

MACBETH   And Thane of Cawdor too; went it not so?

BANQUO   To the self-same tune and words. Who's here?
[Enter ROSS and ANGUS]

ROSS   The king hath happily receiv'd, Macbeth,   90
The news of thy success; and when he reads
Thy personal venture in the rebels' fight,
His wonders and his praises do contend
Which should be thine or his. Silenc'd with that,
In viewing o'er the rest o' the self-same day,   95
He finds thee in the stout Norweyan ranks,
Nothing afeard of what thyself didst make,
Strange images of death. As thick as hail
Came post with post, and every one did bear
Thy praises in his kingdom's great defence,   100
And pour'd them down before him.

SECOND WITCH	You will be less fortunate than he, but much more content.
THIRD WITCH	You will sire a royal dynasty, but you won't be a king. So, welcome to you both, Macbeth and Banquo.
FIRST WITCH	Banquo and Macbeth, greetings!
MACBETH	Wait. You haven't said enough. Tell me more. I became Lord of Glamis after Sinel died, but how did I become Lord of Cawdor? Lord Cawdor is still living and thriving. And how can I be king? I can't believe that prophecy any more than I can believe that I am Lord of Cawdor. Tell me where you got this information. Why did you stop us on this war-torn plain with these predictions? I demand that you tell me. *[Witches vanish]*
BANQUO	These witches disappeared like bubbles. Where did they go?
MACBETH	Into the air. They seemed like flesh, but they dissolved like a breath on the wind. I wish that they had stayed.
BANQUO	Did we really see them or have we eaten a poisonous plant that makes us see illusions?
MACBETH	They said that your children will be kings.
BANQUO	They said that you will be king.
MACBETH	And didn't they also say that I would be Lord of Cawdor?
BANQUO	That's exactly what they said. Who is coming? *[Enter ROSS and ANGUS]*
ROSS	King Duncan is delighted with your combat victories, Macbeth. And when he learns how ably you fought the rebels, he can't decide who deserves the praise, you or himself. In thinking over the day's battles, he is speechless. He is amazed that you fought the Norwegian army without fearing the day's great slaughter. Relay riders poured into camp with news of your defense of Duncan's kingdom.

ANGUS   We are sent
To give thee from our royal master thanks;
Only to herald thee into his sight,
Not pay thee.

ROSS   And, for an earnest of a greater honour,   105
He bade me, from him, call thee Thane of Cawdor:
In which addition, hail, most worthy thane!
For it is thine.

BANQUO   What! can the devil speak true?

MACBETH   The Thane of Cawdor lives: why do you dress me
In borrow'd robes?

ANGUS   Who was the thane lives yet;   110
But under heavy judgment bears that life
Which he deserves to lose. Whether he was combin'd
With those of Norway, or did line the rebel
With hidden help or vantage, or that with both
He labour'd in his country's wrack, I know not;   115
But treasons capital, confess'd and prov'd,
Have overthrown him.

MACBETH   *[Aside]* Glamis, and Thane of Cawdor:
The greatest is behind.
[To ROSS and ANGUS] Thanks for your pains.
[To BANQUO] Do you not hope your children shall be kings,
When those that give the Thane of Cawdor to me   120
Promis'd no less to them?

BANQUO   That, trusted home,
Might yet enkindle you unto the crown,
Besides the Thane of Cawdor. But 'tis strange:
And oftentimes, to win us to our harm,
The instruments of darkness tell us truths,   125
Win us with honest trifles, to betray's
In deepest consequence.
Cousins, a word, I pray you.

ACT I

| ANGUS | He sent us to thank you and to bring you to his court. |

| ROS | He asked me to award you the title of Lord of Cawdor, which you deserve. |

| BANQUO | Did the three witches predict correctly? |

| MACBETH | Lord Cawdor is still alive. Why do you confer his title on me? |

| ANGUS | He is alive, but he is condemned to death and no longer deserves to be called "lord." I don't know why or how he allied with Norway, but I do know he is a traitor. He has confessed to treason, a capital offense. |

| MACBETH | *[To himself]* I am Lord of Glamis and Cawdor: the best part has not happened yet. *[To ROSS and ANGUS]* Thanks for your long ride to deliver the news. *[To BANQUO]* Aren't you excited that your children will be kings? The witches correctly predicted that I would be Lord of Cawdor. |

| BANQUO | If they were telling the truth, you may hope that you will eventually wear Scotland's crown as well as the title of Lord of Cawdor. Often, evil lures us by telling the truth and by giving us rewards that destroy us. Friends, let me speak with you. |

MACBETH   *[Aside]* Two truths are told,
As happy prologues to the swelling act
Of the imperial theme. I thank you, gentlemen.   130
[Aside] This supernatural soliciting
Cannot be ill, cannot be good; if ill,
Why hath it given me earnest of success,
Commencing in a truth? I am Thane of Cawdor:
If good, why do I yield to that suggestion   135
Whose horrid image doth unfix my hair
And make my seated heart knock at my ribs,
Against the use of nature? Present fears
Are less than horrible imaginings;
My thought, whose murder yet is but fantastical,   140
Shakes so my single state of man that function
Is smother'd in surmise, and nothing is
But what is not.

BANQUO   Look, how our partner's rapt.

MACBETH   *[Aside]* If chance will have me king,
why, chance may crown me,
Without my stir.

BANQUO   New honours come upon him,   145
Like our strange garments, cleave not to their mould
But with the aid of use.

MACBETH   *[Aside]* Come what come may,
Time and the hour runs through the roughest day.

BANQUO   Worthy Macbeth, we stay upon your leisure.

MACBETH   Give me your favour: my dull brain was wrought   150
With things forgotten. Kind gentlemen, your pains
Are register'd where every day I turn
The leaf to read them. Let us toward the king.
Think upon what hath chanc'd; and, at more time,
The interim having weigh'd it, let us speak   155
Our free hearts each to other.

BANQUO   Very gladly.

MACBETH   Till then, enough. Come, friends.
[Exeunt]

MACBETH	*[To himself]* The witches have made two true predictions that imply that I will be king. Thank you, Angus and Ross. This magic prophecy is not evil or good. If it were evil, why did it tell the truth about my success in battle? I am truly promoted to Lord of Cawdor. If the prophecy is good, why does it give me thoughts that prickle my scalp and make my heart thump? My fears are real that I will murder Duncan. The prospect of killing the king confuses and unnerves me.
BANQUO	Notice how deep in thought Macbeth seems.
MACBETH	*[To himself]* If luck will make me king, then I may not have to do anything to acquire the crown of Scotland.
BANQUO	Macbeth is pondering his new honor, which won't seem normal until he has been Lord of Cawdor for a while.
MACBETH	*[To himself]* Whatever happens, I must live out the time until I know for sure.
BANQUO	Macbeth, we are waiting for you.
MACBETH	Forgive my musing. I was thinking about something I had forgotten. Sirs, your mission has seized my thoughts. Let us join King Duncan. We should think over the day's events. We can talk about them later.
BANQUO	That's a good idea.
MACBETH	Let's stop our conversation and set off for camp. *[They depart]*

ACT I

TRANSLATION

ACT I, SCENE 4

Forres. A room in the palace.

[Flourish. Enter DUNCAN, MALCOLM, DONALBAIN, LENNOX, and Attendants]

DUNCAN	Is execution done on Cawdor? Are not Those in commission yet return'd?
MALCOLM	My liege,

They are not yet come back; but I have spoke
With one that saw him die; who did report
That very frankly he confess'd his treasons,   5
Implor'd your highness' pardon and set forth
A deep repentance. Nothing in his life
Became him like the leaving it; he died
As one that had been studied in his death
To throw away the dearest thing he ow'd,   10
As 'twere a careless trifle.

DUNCAN   There's no art
To find the mind's construction in the face:
He was a gentleman on whom I built
An absolute trust.
[Enter MACBETH, BANQUO, ROSS, and ANGUS]
                                            O worthiest cousin!
The sin of my ingratitude even now   15
Was heavy on me. Thou art so far before
That swiftest wing of recompense is slow
To overtake thee; would thou hadst less deserv'd,
That the proportion both of thanks and payment
Might have been mine! only I have left to say,   20
More is thy due than more than all can pay.

MACBETH   The service and the loyalty I owe,
In doing it, pays itself. Your highness, part
Is to receive our duties; and our duties
Are to your throne and state, children and servants;   25
Which do but what they should, by doing everything
Safe toward your love and honour.

DUNCAN   Welcome hither:
I have begun to plant thee, and will labour
To make thee full of growing. Noble Banquo,
That hast no less deserv'd, nor must be known   30
No less to have done so, let me infold thee
And hold thee to my heart.

ORIGINAL

ACT I, SCENE 4

At Duncan's palace in Forres.

[A trumpet fanfare. KING DUNCAN, his sons DONALBAIN and MALCOLM, the nobleman LENNOX, and servants enter]

DUNCAN   Has Cawdor been executed? Have his executioners returned?

MALCOLM   My king, the executioners have not returned; but I talked with an eyewitness who reported that Lord Cawdor confessed to treason, begged the king's pardon, and repented of his crimes. He died nobly like a man who gives up life willingly and freely, as though it were nothing.

DUNCAN   There was no way to know he was a traitor by looking at him. He behaved like a trustworthy gentleman. *[Enter MACBETH, BANQUO, ROSS, and ANGUS]* Noble Macbeth, I am eager to express my thanks to you. You are so deserving of reward that I can't repay quickly enough. I owe you much more.

MACBETH   I am content with performing the service that I owe my king. Your highness, I accept my obligation to you and to Scotland; I did what a loyal subject should do to express love and honor to the king.

DUNCAN   Welcome. I placed you in an important position and will work toward grooming your career. Banquo, you are also deserving of honor. Let me embrace you.

TRANSLATION

BANQUO   There if I grow,
The harvest is your own.

DUNCAN   My plenteous joys
Wanton in fulness, seek to hide themselves
In drops of sorrow. Sons, kinsmen, thanes,   35
And you whose places are the nearest, know
We will establish our estate upon
Our eldest, Malcolm, whom we name hereafter
The Prince of Cumberland; which honour must
Not unaccompanied invest him only,   40
But signs of nobleness, like stars, shall shine
On all deservers. From hence to Inverness,
And bind us further to you.

MACBETH   The rest is labour, which is not us'd for you:
I'll be myself the harbinger, and make joyful   45
The hearing of my wife with your approach;
So, humbly take my leave.

DUNCAN   My worthy Cawdor!

MACBETH   *[Aside]* The Prince of Cumberland! that is a step
On which I must fall down, or else o'er-leap,
For in my way it lies. Stars, hide your fires!   50
Let not light see my black and deep desires;
The eye wink at the hand; yet let that be
Which the eye fears, when it is done, to see. *[Exit]*

DUNCAN   True, worthy Banquo; he is full so valiant,
And in his commendations I am fed;   55
It is a banquet to me. Let's after him,
Whose care is gone before to bid us welcome:
It is a peerless kinsman. *[Flourish. Exeunt]*

BANQUO   If I advance in honors, you deserve the credit.

DUNCAN   I am so pleased that I am weeping. Princes, relatives,
lords, and courtiers, I confer on Malcolm, my oldest son,
the title Prince of Cumberland, an indication that he will
succeed me on Scotland's throne. Malcolm's honor accom-
panies rewards to all who deserve royal praise. Let us go
to Macbeth's castle at Inverness as his guest.

MACBETH   I cannot rest from serving you. I will ride ahead and
inform my wife that you are coming to the castle.
On my way out, I bow to your majesty.

DUNCAN   You are well deserving of the title of Lord Cawdor!

MACBETH   *[To himself]* Malcolm is heir to the throne! that is an
obstacle that I must fall against or overcome to make my
way to Scotland's throne. Stars, darken my evil thoughts
and conceal what my hand must do, but let me see the
outcome when I have committed the crime. *[He departs]*

DUNCAN   You are right, Banquo, that Macbeth deserves reward.
I feel nourished by his deeds as though I had eaten a
banquet. Let's follow Macbeth, who has ridden ahead to
prepare for our welcome. He is a cousin without equal.
[A trumpet fanfare. They depart]

TRANSLATION

ACT I, SCENE 5

Inverness. Macbeth's castle.

[Enter LADY MACBETH, reading a letter]

LADY MACBETH   *They met me in the day of success; and*
I have learned by the perfectest report, they have more
in them than mortal knowledge. When I burned in desire
to question them further, they made themselves air, into
which they vanished. Whiles I stood rapt in the wonder   5
of it, came missives from the king, who all-hailed
me 'Thane of Cawdor,' by which title, before, these
weird sisters saluted me, and referred me to the
coming on of time, with, 'Hail, king that shalt be!'
This have I thought good to deliver thee, my dearest   10
partner of greatness, that thou mightest not lose the
dues of rejoicing, but being ignorant of what greatness
is promised thee. Lay it to thy heart, and farewell.
Glamis thou art, and Cawdor; and shalt be
What thou art promis'd. Yet do I fear thy nature;   15
It is too full o' the milk of human kindness
To catch the nearest way; thou wouldst be great,
Art not without ambition, but without
The illness should attend it; what thou wouldst highly,
That thou wouldst holily; wouldst not play false,   20
And yet wouldst wrongly win; thou'dst have, great Glamis,
That which cries, 'Thus thou must do, if thou have it;'
And that which rather thou dost fear to do
Than wishest should be undone. Hie thee hither,
That I may pour my spirits in thine ear,   25
And chastise with the valour of my tongue
All that impedes thee from the golden round,
Which fate and metaphysical aid doth seem
To have thee crown'd withal.
[Enter a Messenger]
                                        What is your tidings?

MESSENGER   The king comes here to-night.

ACT I, SCENE 5

Macbeth's castle at Inverness, which is west of Forres.

[Enter LADY MACBETH, reading a letter]

LADY MACBETH "The witches reported the day's victory; and I learned from their magic a wonderful prophecy. When I tried to learn more, the witches vanished. While I stood gaping, the king's messengers greeted me as Lord of Cawdor, a title that the witches referred to. The trio also predicted that I will be king. I was eager to tell you, my love and wife, that you could enjoy the good news and the prophecy of greatness to come. Treasure the news in your heart. Goodbye."

You are Lord of Glamis and Cawdor and you will be king as the witches predicted. Yet, I am afraid that you are too compassionate to take shortcuts to the throne. You are ambitious for greatness, but you lack the conniving to make it happen. You would be royal, but you prefer to win the throne honestly. You don't want to commit crimes, yet you desire to replace Malcolm as Duncan's successor. Lord Glamis, you know you must do wrong to achieve your ambition. You fear to do what you must accomplish to become king. Hurry home so I can twist your thinking with my sharp words toward the obstacles that stand in the way of your crowning, a rise to greatness that destiny and the witches have promised. *[Enter a Messenger]* What is your message?

MESSENGER King Duncan will arrive by tonight.

TRANSLATION

LADY MACBETH   Thou'rt mad to say it!   30
Is not thy master with him? who, were't so,
Would have inform'd for preparation.

MESSENGER   So please you, it is true: our thane is coming;
One of my fellows had the speed of him,
Who, almost dead for breath, had scarcely more
Than would make up his message.

LADY MACBETH   Give him tending;   35
He brings great news. *[Exit Messenger]*
                          The raven himself is hoarse
That croaks the fatal entrance of Duncan
Under my battlements. Come, you spirits
That tend on mortal thoughts! unsex me here,
And fill me from the crown to the toe top full   40
Of direst cruelty; make thick my blood,
Stop up the access and passage to remorse,
That no compunctious visitings of nature
Shake my fell purpose, nor keep peace between
The effect and it! Come to my woman's breasts,   45
And take my milk for gall, you murdering ministers,
Wherever in your sightless substances
You wait on nature's mischief! Come, thick night,
And pall thee in the dunnest smoke of hell,
That my keen knife see not the wound it makes,   50
Nor heaven peep through the blanket of the dark,
To cry, 'Hold, hold!'
[Enter MACBETH]
                          Great Glamis! worthy Cawdor!
Greater than both, by the all-hail hereafter!
Thy letters have transported me beyond
This ignorant present, and I feel now   55
The future in the instant.

MACBETH   My dearest love,
Duncan comes here to-night.

LADY MACBETH   And when goes hence?

MACBETH   To-morrow, as he purposes.

LADY MACBETH   You are insane. Isn't Macbeth with the king? If Macbeth knew the king's plans, he could have had me prepare for the visit.

MESSENGER   Yes, Lord Macbeth is coming. Another messenger outrode him and, completely out of breath, could barely deliver his message.

LADY MACBETH   Let the messenger rest. He brought good news. *[The messenger goes out]* The crow that reports Duncan's arrival is hoarse from delivering the deadly message that the king is staying at Macbeth's castle. Come, guardians of the human mind, strip away womanly thoughts and fill me from head to toe with savagery. Thicken my blood and halt the flow of regret. I want no visits of conscience to distract me from my evil plan. Replace my breast milk with bitterness, you murderous spirits, wherever you lurk in darkness before committing evil. Come, dark night, and cover yourself in hellish fog so that I can't see the knife wound that I inflict nor hear a cry from heaven to halt. *[Enter MACBETH]* Lord of Glamis and Cawdor! You are predicted to be even greater. Your letters have whisked me away from the present to a future that will soon come true.

MACBETH   Dearest wife, King Duncan will spend the night here.

LADY MACBETH   When does he plan to leave?

MACBETH   He expects to leave tomorrow.

LADY MACBETH   O! never
    Shall sun that morrow see.
    Your face, my thane, is as a book where men   60
    May read strange matters. To beguile the time,
    Look like the time; bear welcome in your eye,
    Your hand, your tongue: look like the innocent flower,
    But be the serpent under 't. He that's coming
    Must be provided for; and you shall put   65
    This night's great business into my dispatch;
    Which shall to all our nights and days to come
    Give solely sovereign sway and masterdom.

MACBETH   We will speak further.

LADY MACBETH   Only look up clear;
    To alter favour ever is to fear.   70
    Leave all the rest to me. *[Exeunt]*

LADY MACBETH   Tomorrow will never come for Duncan. Your expression gives away your intent to commit a crime. Pass the time by acting like a host. Welcome the king with gestures and words. Look innocent while concealing your murderous intent. You must prepare for a royal visit; and you will leave to me the murder plot, which will reward us in the future with Scotland's royal power.

MACBETH   We will talk more of this later.

LADY MACBETH   Look innocent to conceal your intent. Leave the rest of the plot to me. *[They depart]*

ACT I, SCENE 6

The same. Before the castle.

[Hautboys and torches. Enter DUNCAN, MALCOLM, DONALBAIN, BANQUO,
LENNOX, MACDUFF, ROSS, ANGUS and Attendants]

DUNCAN   This castle hath a pleasant seat; the air
Nimbly and sweetly recommends itself
Unto our gentle senses.

BANQUO   This guest of summer,
The temple-haunting martlet, does approve
By his lov'd mansionry that the heaven's breath   5
Smells wooingly here: no jutty, frieze,
Buttress, nor coign of vantage, but this bird
Hath made his pendent bed and procreant cradle:
Where they most breed and haunt, I have observ'd
The air is delicate.
[Enter LADY MACBETH]

DUNCAN   See, see, our honour'd hostess!   10
The love that follows us sometime is our trouble,
Which still we thank as love. Herein I teach you
How you shall bid God 'eyld us for your pains,
And thank us for your trouble.

LADY MACBETH   All our service,
In every point twice done, and then done double,   15
Were poor and single business, to contend
Against those honours deep and broad wherewith
Your majesty loads our house: for those of old,
And the late dignities heap'd up to them,
We rest your hermits.

DUNCAN   Where's the Thane of Cawdor?   20
We cours'd him at the heels, and had a purpose
To be his purveyor; but he rides well,
And his great love, sharp as his spur, hath holp him
To his home before us. Fair and noble hostess,
We are your guest to-night.

ACT I, SCENE 6

The same. Before the castle.

[Oboes and torchlight. Enter KING DUNCAN, princes MALCOLM and DONALBAIN, lords BANQUO, LENNOX, MACDUFF, ROSS, and ANGUS, and servants]

DUNCAN   Macbeth's castle is pleasing; I am pleased to stop in this serene setting.

BANQUO   The martin, a summer bird, chooses Macbeth's castle for its pure air. The bird has built nests on the nooks and crannies of its architecture. *[Enter LADY MACBETH]*

DUNCAN   Here is our hostess, Lady Macbeth. Sometimes the love of our subjects is troublesome, but we are grateful for it. I thank you for treating us to your hospitality.

LADY MACBETH My service, even doubled and quadrupled, is far less than the honor you bestow by visiting our home. For former kindnesses and for the recent honors you gave Macbeth, we offer you our prayers.

DUNCAN   We followed him closely and intended to arrive before him, but his love for you has sped him home before us. Beautiful and noble hostess, we will remain with you tonight.

LADY MACBETH　　　　　　　　　　　　　　Your servants ever　　　25
Have theirs, themselves, and what is theirs, in compt,
To make their audit at your highness' pleasure,
Still to return your own.

DUNCAN　　　　　　　　　　　　　　　　Give me your hand;
Conduct me to mine host: we love him highly,
And shall continue our graces towards him.　　　30
By your leave, hostess. *[Exeunt]*

LADY MACBETH Your subjects hold themselves and their homes and goods at your pleasure and offer their all for your inspection and use.

DUNCAN Give me your hand and lead me to Macbeth. We treasure him and shall continue valuing him. With your permission, hostess. *[They go out]*

ACT I

ACT I, SCENE 7

The same. A room in the castle.

[Hautboys and torches. Enter, and pass over the stage, a Sewer, and divers Servants with dishes and service. Then, enter MACBETH]

MACBETH	If it were done when 'tis done, then 'twere well
	It were done quickly; if the assassination
	Could trammel up the consequence, and catch
	With his surcease success: that but this blow
	Might be the be-all and the end-all. Here,

If it were done when 'tis done, then 'twere well
It were done quickly; if the assassination
Could trammel up the consequence, and catch
With his surcease success: that but this blow
Might be the be-all and the end-all. Here,   5
But here, upon this bank and shoal of time,
We'd jump the life to come. But in these cases
We still have judgment here; that we but teach
Bloody instructions, which, being taught, return
To plague the inventor; this even-handed justice   10
Commends the ingredients of our poison'd chalice
To our own lips. He's here in double trust:
First, as I am his kinsman and his subject,
Strong both against the deed; then, as his host,
Who should against his murderer shut the door,   15
Not bear the knife myself. Besides, this Duncan
Hath borne his faculties so meek, hath been
So clear in his great office, that his virtues
Will plead like angels trumpet-tongu'd against
The deep damnation of his taking-off;   20
And pity, like a naked new-born babe,
Striding the blast, or heaven's cherubin, hors'd
Upon the sightless couriers of the air,
Shall blow the horrid deed in every eye,
That tears shall drown the wind. I have no spur   25
To prick the sides of my intent, but only
Vaulting ambition, which o'er-leaps itself
And falls on the other—
[Enter LADY MACBETH]
How now! what news?

LADY MACBETH   He has almost supp'd: why have you left the chamber?

MACBETH   Hath he ask'd for me?

LADY MACBETH   Know you not he has?   30

MACBETH   We will proceed no further in this business:
He hath honour'd me of late; and I have bought
Golden opinions from all sorts of people,
Which would be worn now in their newest gloss,
Not cast aside so soon.

ORIGINAL

ACT I, SCENE 7

Immediately after in a room at Inverness Castle.

[Oboes and torchlight. Entering and crossing the stage are the butler and servants bearing food and drink. MACBETH enters]

MACBETH If it requires only one crime, then I want to finish it quickly. If assassination can assure my destiny and his death bring me success, then I want this attack to end my crimes. We stand in earthly time and attempt to leap over judgment in eternity. Judgment awaits the assassin on earth and threatens punishment for the killer. Justice serves up the same poison to us that we offer to our victims. For two reasons, I shouldn't kill Duncan, who is both my cousin and my king. Both relationships argue against assassination. Also, I am his host and protector who should shield him from harm and should, myself, not endanger him. Also, King Duncan has been so mild and good a ruler that his murder will condemn forever his killer. News of his assassination will spread to his subjects, who will weep for his undeserved passing. I can think of no reason for my plot except my ambition for the throne. My leap at ambition will cause me to overshoot the throne and fall on the other side. *[Enter LADY MACBETH]* What is happening?

LADY MACBETH He is finishing dinner. Why have you left the dining room?

MACBETH Has he summoned me?

LADY MACBETH Don't you know that he is asking for you?

MACBETH We must abandon this murder plot. He has rewarded me today and elevated my reputation. I must enjoy my rewards rather than dishonor them.

LADY MACBETH   Was the hope drunk,   35
Wherein you dress'd yourself? hath it slept since,
And wakes it now, to look so green and pale
At what it did so freely? From this time
Such I account thy love. Art thou afeard
To be the same in thine own act and valour   40
As thou art in desire? Wouldst thou have that
Which thou esteem'st the ornament of life,
And live a coward in thine own esteem,
Letting 'I dare not' wait upon 'I would,'
Like the poor cat i' the adage?

MACBETH   Prithee, peace   45
I dare do all that may become a man;
Who dares do more is none.

LADY MACBETH   What beast was't, then,
That made you break this enterprise to me?
When you durst do it, then you were a man;
And, to be more than what you were, you would   50
Be so much more the man. Nor time nor place
Did then adhere, and yet you would make both:
They have made themselves, and that their fitness now
Does unmake you. I have given suck, and know
How tender 'tis to love the babe that milks me: 55
I would, while it was smiling in my face,
Have pluck'd my nipple from his boneless gums,
And dash'd the brains out, had I so sworn as you
Have done to this.

MACBETH   If we should fail,—

LADY MACBETH   We fail?
But screw your courage to the sticking-place,   60
And we'll not fail. When Duncan is asleep,
Whereto the rather shall his day's hard journey
Soundly invite him, his two chamberlains
Will I with wine and wassail so convince,
That memory, the warder of the brain,   65
Shall be a fume, and the receipt of reason
A limbeck only; when in swinish sleep
Their drenched natures lie, as in a death,
What cannot you and I perform upon
The unguarded Duncan? what not put upon   70
His spongy officers, who shall bear the guilt
Of our great quell?

ORIGINAL

LADY MACBETH Was your deceit short-lived, like a drunkard who wakes up ill and sorry for his behavior the night before? From now on, I shall consider your devotion undependable. Are you afraid to put your plan into action? Are you too cowardly to seize the height of your ambition, like a cat that is afraid to seize a fish lest he wet his feet?

MACBETH Quiet, please. I do what a man must. Anyone who does more is less than a man.

LADY MACBETH What kind of animal proposed this plot to me? If you do what you plan, you are manly. By attaining your ambition, you are even greater. The opportunity won't wait. The right place and time have scared you. I have suckled a baby and know its innocence and sweetness, but if I swore to dash out its brains, I would do it.

MACBETH What if we fail?

LADY MACBETH Fail? Summon your courage and we won't fail. When Duncan falls asleep from his day's labors, I will make his servants drunk on wine. When the two servants are dead drunk, you and I can do what we will to Duncan. We can easily shift the blame to his sodden servants.

MACBETH   Bring forth men-children only;
For thy undaunted mettle should compose
Nothing but males. Will it not be receiv'd,
When we have mark'd with blood those sleepy two   75
Of his own chamber and us'd their very daggers,
That they have done't?

LADY MACBETH   Who dares receive it other,
As we shall make our griefs and clamour roar
Upon his death?

MACBETH   I am settled, and bend up
Each corporal agent to this terrible feat.   80
Away, and mock the time with fairest show:
False face must hide what the false heart doth know.
[Exeunt]

MACBETH	You are so hardened that you should bear only boy babies. Can't we shift blame to the servants by using their daggers and smearing the men with blood?
LADY MACBETH	No one will challenge the story if we raise an outcry and pretend to grieve for the dead king.
MACBETH	I agree. I will dedicate myself to this terrible crime. Let's join the company and pretend to have a good time. We must hide our deceit under our masks of hospitality. *[They depart]*

ACT II, SCENE 1

Inverness. Court within the castle.

[Enter BANQUO and FLEANCE, with a Servant bearing a torch before him]

BANQUO   How goes the night, boy?

FLEANCE   The moon is down; I have not heard the clock.

BANQUO   And she goes down at twelve.

FLEANCE   I take 't, 'tis later, sir.

BANQUO   Hold, take my sword. There's husbandry in heaven;
Their candles are all out. Take thee that too.   5
A heavy summons lies like lead upon me,
And yet I would not sleep: merciful powers!
Restrain in me the cursed thoughts that nature
Gives way to in repose.
[Enter MACBETH, and a Servant with a torch]
                            Give me my sword.—
Who's there?   10

MACBETH   A friend.

BANQUO   What, sir! not yet at rest? The king's a-bed:
He hath been in unusual pleasure, and
Sent forth great largess to your offices.
This diamond he greets your wife withal,   15
By the name of most kind hostess; and shut up
In measureless content.

MACBETH   Being unprepar'd,
Our will became the servant to defect,
Which else should free have wrought.

BANQUO   All's well.
I dreamt last night of the three weird sisters: 20
To you they have show'd some truth.

MACBETH   I think not of them:
Yet, when we can entreat an hour to serve,
We would spend it in some words upon that business,
If you would grant the time.

BANQUO   At your kind'st leisure.

MACBETH   If you shall cleave to my consent, when'tis,   25
It shall make honour for you.

ACT II, SCENE 1

The main hall in Macbeth's castle at Inverness.

[Enter BANQUO *and* FLEANCE, *with a Servant bearing a torch before him]*

BANQUO   How late is it, son?

FLEANCE   The moon has set. I haven't heard the clock chime.

BANQUO   The moon sets at midnight.

FLEANCE   I think it's after midnight, sir.

BANQUO   Wait, take my sword. The sky shows thrift by putting out its lights. Take that *[a dagger]* too. I am very weary, but I can't sleep. Merciful heaven, rid me of the bad thoughts that bother my rest. *[Enter* MACBETH, *and a Servant with a torch]* Hand me my sword. Who's coming?

MACBETH   Your friend.

BANQUO   Haven't you retired yet? The king is sleeping. He has been in an unusually good mood and has sent great gifts to your servants. For Lady Macbeth's hospitality, he has given her a diamond and has gone to bed well contented.

MACBETH   If we had known the king was coming here, we might have planned a better welcome.

BANQUO   It was a good evening. I dreamed last night of the three witches: They predicted correctly your advancement to Thane of Cawdor.

MACBETH   If you would grant the time. I haven't given any thought to the witches: However, when we have a free hour, we should discuss their prophecy, if you can spare the time.

BANQUO   Whenver you're ready.

MACBETH   If you remain true to me, when I advance, you will gain honors.

BANQUO   So I lose none
                    In seeking to augment it, but still keep
                    My bosom franchis'd and allegiance clear,
                    I shall be counsell'd.

MACBETH   Good repose the while!

BANQUO   Thanks, sir: the like to you.   30
                    [Exeunt BANQUO *and* FLEANCE*]*

MACBETH   Go bid thy mistress, when my drink is ready
                    She strike upon the bell. Get thee to bed.
                    [Exit Servant]
                    Is this a dagger which I see before me,
                    The handle toward my hand? Come, let me clutch thee:
                    I have thee not, and yet I see thee still.   35
                    Art thou not, fatal vision, sensible
                    To feeling as to sight? or art thou but
                    A dagger of the mind, a false creation,
                    Proceeding from the heat-oppressed brain?
                    I see thee yet, in form as palpable   40
                    As this which now I draw.
                    Thou marshall'st me the way that I was going;
                    And such an instrument I was to use.
                    Mine eyes are made the fools o' the other senses,
                    Or else worth all the rest: I see thee still;   45
                    And on thy blade and dudgeon gouts of blood
                    Which was not so before. There's no such thing:
                    It is the bloody business which informs
                    Thus to mine eyes. Now o'er the one half-world
                    Nature seems dead, and wicked dreams abuse   50
                    The curtain'd sleep; witchcraft celebrates
                    Pale Hecate's offerings; and wither'd murder,
                    Alarum'd by his sentinel, the wolf,
                    Whose howl's his watch, thus with his stealthy pace,
                    With Tarquin's ravishing strides, toward his design   55
                    Moves like a ghost. Thou sure and firm-set earth,
                    Hear not my steps, which way they walk, for fear
                    Thy very stones prate of my whereabout,
                    And take the present horror from the time,
                    Which now suits with it. Whiles I threat, he lives: 60
                    Words to the heat of deeds too cold breath gives.
                    [A bell rings]
                    I go, and it is done; the bell invites me.
                    Hear it not, Duncan; for it is a knell
                    That summons thee to heaven or to hell.

ORIGINAL

BANQUO   Only if I lose none of my honor in trying to increase it, but keep myself blameless and my loyalty true, I will hear your advice.

MACBETH   Until then, rest easy.

BANQUO   Thanks, sir, and the same to you. *[BANQUO and his son FLEANCE depart]*

MACBETH   Tell my wife to ring the bell when my drink is ready. You may retire. *[Exit Servant]* Can I be seeing a dagger in the air with the handle at my hand? Come, let me hold you. I can't touch you, but I still see you. Are you a death omen that I can touch as well as see, or are you an illusion that I imagine because of anxiety? I still see you—as real as my own weapon that I pull from its sheath. You point me the way to my mission and represent the weapon I was going to use against Duncan. My eyes are deceiving me or else they show me a true vision. I still see you. On your blade and handle are drops of blood that I didn't see at first. This is unreal. It is the murder plot that tricks my eyes. Now over half the world, nature seems dead and evil dreams ruin my night's sleep. Sorcery flourishes in the pale light of Hecate, the moon goddess. And the image of a shrunken corpse, summoned by a wolf, watchman of murder, creeps like a ghost with the horrid advance of Tarquin, the Etruscan murderer-king. Oh, earth, hear nothing of my foosteps lest stones give away my advance in the dark, a suitable time for horrid deeds. While I plan the murder, Duncan remains alive. Talking about killing him cools my passion for committing the crime. *[A bell rings]* I am going to finish the deed; the signal summons me. Duncan, may you hear no bell that indicates the end of your life and your soul's departure to heaven or hell.

ACT II

ACT II, SCENE 2

The same.

[Enter LADY MACBETH]

LADY MACBETH	That which hath made them drunk hath made me bold,
	What hath quench'd them hath given me fire. Hark! Peace!
	It was the owl that shriek'd, the fatal bellman,
	Which gives the stern'st good-night. He is about it:
	The doors are open, and the surfeited grooms 5
	Do mock their charge with snores: I have drugg'd
	their possets,
	That death and nature do contend about them,
	Whether they live or die.

MACBETH	*[Within]* Who's there? what, ho!

LADY MACBETH	Alack! I am afraid they have awak'd.
	And 'tis not done; the attempt and not the deed 10
	Confounds us. Hark! I laid their daggers ready;
	He could not miss them. Had he not resembled
	My father as he slept, I had done 't. *[Enter MACBETH]*
	My husband!

MACBETH	I have done the deed. Didst thou not hear a noise 15

LADY MACBETH	I heard the owl scream and the crickets cry.
	Did not you speak?

MACBETH	When?

LADY MACBETH	Now.

MACBETH	As I descended?

LADY MACBETH	Ay.

MACBETH	Hark!
	Who lies i' the second chamber?

LADY MACBETH	Donalbain. 20

MACBETH	*[Looking on his hands]* This is a sorry sight.

LADY MACBETH	A foolish thought to say a sorry sight.

ACT II, SCENE 2

The same.

[Enter LADY MACBETH]

LADY MACBETH   The wine that intoxicated the servants has made me bold and fiery. What was that? Shh! It was the shriek of an owl, the ominous night bird that prophesies death. Macbeth is killing Duncan: The chamber doors are open and the drunken servants snore rather than keep watch. I have drugged their night drinks so that they sleep like the dead.

MACBETH   *[Within]* Who's there? What's that noise?

LADY MACBETH   Oh, no! I am afraid the servants have awakened before Macbeth has stabbed Duncan. We will be found guilty of attempted murder of the king. Look! I placed the servants' daggers where Macbeth would find them. If Duncan had not looked so much like my father in sleep, I would have murdered him myself. *[Enter MACBETH]* Macbeth!

MACBETH   I have carried out the murder plot. Did you hear something?

LADY MACBETH   I heard the cry of an owl and crickets chirping. Did you say something?

MACBETH   When?

LADY MACBETH   Just now.

MACBETH   When I came down the stairs?

LADY MACBETH   Yes.

MACBETH   Listen! Who is sleeping in the second bedroom?

LADY MACBETH   Donalbain, the king's son.

MACBETH   *[Looking at his hands]* My bloody hands are a sorry sight.

LADY MACBETH   It is silly to say "sorry."

ACT II

TRANSLATION

MACBETH	There's one did laugh in 's sleep, and one cried 'Murder!'
	That they did wake each other: I stood and heard them;
	But they did say their prayers, and address'd them 25
	Again to sleep.
LADY MACBETH	There are two lodg'd together.
MACBETH	One cried 'God bless us!' and 'Amen' the other:
	As they had seen me with these hangman's hands.
	Listening their fear, I could not say 'Amen,'
	When they did say 'God bless us!'
LADY MACBETH	Consider it not so deeply. 30
MACBETH	But wherefore could not I pronounce 'Amen'?
	I had most need of blessing, and 'Amen'
	Stuck in my throat.
LADY MACBETH	These deeds must not be thought
	After these ways; so, it will make us mad.
MACBETH	Methought I heard a voice cry 'Sleep no more! 35
	Macbeth does murder sleep,' the innocent sleep,
	Sleep that knits up the ravell'd sleave of care,
	The death of each day's life, sore labour's bath,
	Balm of hurt minds, great nature's second course,
	Chief nourisher in life's feast,—
LADY MACBETH	What do you mean? 40
MACBETH	Still it cried, 'Sleep no more!' to all the house:
	'Glamis hath murder'd sleep, and therefore Cawdor
	Shall sleep no more, Macbeth shall sleep no more!'
LADY MACBETH	Who was it that thus cried? Why, worthy thane
	You do unbend your noble strength to think 45
	So brainsickly of things. Go get some water,
	And wash this filthy witness from your hand.
	Why did you bring these daggers from the place?
	They must lie there: go carry them, and smear
	The sleepy grooms with blood.
MACBETH	I'll go no more: 50
	I am afraid to think what I have done;
	Look on 't again I dare not.

MACBETH	Someone laughed in his sleep and another person called out "Murder!" The two sleepers woke each other. I stood there and listened to them; but they said their prayers and went back to sleep.
LADY MACBETH	The two voices come from the same room.
MACBETH	One said "God bless us!" and the other replied "Amen" as though the two had seen me with an assassin's hands. When I listened to them, I could not say "Amen" when they said "God bless us!"
LADY MACBETH	Forget it.
MACBETH	But why could I not say "Amen" when I was most in need of God's blessing. The "Amen" stuck in my throat.
LADY MACBETH	Don't think of the murder in religious terms. Your moralizing will drive us crazy.
MACBETH	I thought I heard a voice cry "There will be no more sleep because Macbeth has murdered it," the peaceful slumber that soothes worry and rounds out the day, slumber that restores the body from work and stress, nature's fuel for a busy life.
LADY MACBETH	What are you talking about?
MACBETH	The voice cried again, "Sleep no more!" to the household. It said, "The thane of Glamis has destroyed sleep; the Thane of Cawdor shall not rest. Macbeth will never enjoy a peaceful sleep!"
LADY MACBETH	What voice cried out to you? You are a brave warrior, yet you make yourself weak with such sick imaginings. Bring some water to wash the bloody evidence from your hand. Why did you remove the daggers from the murder scene? Take them back to Duncan's bedroom and wipe the blood on the sleeping servants.
MACBETH	I won't go: I am afraid to think of my crime. I don't dare look at the corpse again.

ACT II

LADY MACBETH   Infirm of purpose!
Give me the daggers. The sleeping and the dead
Are but as pictures; 'tis the eye of childhood
That fears a painted devil. If he do bleed,   55
I'll gild the faces of the grooms withal;
For it must seem their guilt.
[Exit. Knocking within]

MACBETH   Whence is that knocking?
How is 't with me, when every noise appals me?
What hands are here! Ha! they pluck out mine eyes.
Will all great Neptune's ocean wash this blood   60
Clean from my hand? No, this my hand will rather
The multitudinous seas incarnadine,
Making the green one red.
[Re-enter LADY MACBETH]

LADY MACBETH My hands are of your colour, but I shame
To wear a heart so white.— *[Knocking within]* I hear
    a knocking   65
At the south entry; retire we to our chamber;
A little water clears us of this deed;
How easy is it, then! Your constancy
Hath left you unattended. *[Knocking within]* Hark!
    more knocking.
Get on your night-gown, lest occasion call us,   70
And show us to be watchers. Be not lost
So poorly in your thoughts.

MACBETH To know my deed 'twere best not know myself.
[Knocking within]
Wake Duncan with thy knocking! I would thou couldst!
[Exeunt]

LADY MACBETH What a weakling. Hand me the daggers. There is no difference between the look of a corpse and a sleeping man. Your childish fear makes you see evil. If Duncan is bloody, I'll smear his blood on the two servants to make them seem guilty. *[She departs. There is a knock from inside the castle]*

MACBETH Where is that knocking coming from? What is wrong with me that I flinch at every noise? Look at these terrible hands! They destroy my normal vision. Will all the water in the ocean rinse this blood from my hand? No, my hand is so bloody that it will turn seawater red. *[Re-enter LADY MACBETH]*

LADY MACBETH My hands are as bloody as yours, but I would be ashamed to be so terrified. *[Knocking within]* I hear knocking at the southern entrance. Let's get to bed. We can easily wash away evidence of the crime. You have lost your usual composure. *[Knocking within]* Listen! More knocking. Put on your night clothes so no one will summon us and find us still awake. Don't give in to scary imaginings.

MACBETH When I think about what I've done, I don't want to know myself. *[Knocking within]* I wish the knocking could awaken Duncan. *[They go out]*

TRANSLATION

ACT II, SCENE 3

The same.

[Knocking within. Enter a Porter]

PORTER Here's a knocking indeed! If a man were porter of
hell-gate, he should have old turning the key. *[Knocking
within]* Knock, knock, knock! Who's there, i' the name
of Beelzebub? Here's a farmer that hanged himself on the
expectation of plenty; come in time; have napkins   5
enough about you; here you'll sweat for 't. *[Knocking
within]* Knock, knock! Who's there, i' the other devil's
name! Faith, here's an equivocator that could swear in
both the scales against either scale; who committed treason
enough for God's sake, yet could not equivocate to heaven: 10
O! come in, equivocator. *[Knocking within]* Knock, knock,
knock! Who's there? Faith, here's an English tailor come
hither for stealing out of a French hose: come in, tailor;
here you may roast your goose. *[Knocking within]* Knock,
knock; never at quiet! What are you? But this place   15
is too cold for hell. I'll devil-porter it no further: I had
thought to have let in some of all professions, that go
the primrose way to the everlasting bonfire. *[Knocking
within]* Anon, anon! I pray you, remember the porter.
[Opens the gate. Enter MACDUFF and LENNOX]

MACDUFF Was it so late, friend, ere you went to bed,   20
That you do lie so late?

PORTER Faith, sir, we were carousing till the second cock:
and drink, sir, is a great provoker of three things.

MACDUFF What three things does drink especially provoke?

PORTER Marry, sir, nose-painting, sleep, and urine.   25
Lechery, sir, it provokes, and unprovokes; it provokes
the desire, but it takes away the performance:
therefore, much drink may be said to be an equivocator
with lechery: it makes him, and it mars him;
it sets him on, and it takes him off; it persuades   30
him, and disheartens him; makes him stand to, and
not stand to; in conclusion, equivocates him in a
sleep, and, giving him the lie, leaves him.

MACDUFF I believe drink gave thee the lie last night.

ACT II, SCENE 3

The same.

[Knocking from inside the castle. The gatekeeper enters]

PORTER   Yes, it is knocking. If I were hell's gatekeeper, I would
have difficulty turning the key. *[Knocking within]*
Knock, knock, knock! In the name of Satan, who is it?
One likely arrival in hell is the farmer who hanged
himself for hoarding grain in hard times. Did you bring
handkerchiefs? You'll sweat for your sin. *[Knocking within]*
Knock, knock! Who is it, in Satan's name! Truly, here's a
deceiver who could claim both sides of an argument,
who committed treason under a godly oath, but could
not trick his way into heaven. Oh, come in, deceiver.
[Knocking within] Knock, knock, knock! Who's there?
Truly, it's an English tailor who scrimped on the making
of tight pants: come in, tailor, where hell will roast your
goose. *[Knocking within]* Knock, knock; I never get any
rest! Who is it? This castle is too cold to be hell. I'll stop
pretending to be hell's gatekeeper: I was going to keep
naming the types of people who sin all their lives and then
end up in the eternal fire. *[Knocking within]* I'm coming,
I'm coming! Please, don't forget to tip the gatekeeper.
[Opens the gate. Enter MACDUFF and LENNOX]

MACDUFF   Did you go to bed so late that you overslept?

PORTER   Indeed, we celebrated until 2:00 a.m.: alcohol is the cause
of three things.

MACDUFF   What three things does drinking cause?

PORTER   Alcohol causes a red nose, drowsiness, and urine.
It arouses sexual desire, then dampens it; it raises the
urge, but halts the sex act. Thus, alcohol deceives by both
inflaming and subduing desire.

MACDUFF   I think you had too much to drink last night.

PORTER	That it did, sir, i' the very throat on me: but I requited 35 him for his lie; and, I think, being too strong for him, though he took up my legs sometime yet I made a shift to cast him.
MACDUFF	Is thy master stirring? *[Enter MACBETH]* Our knocking has awak'd him; here he comes. 40
LENNOX	Good morrow, noble sir.
MACBETH	Good morrow, both.
MACDUFF	Is the king stirring, worthy thane?
MACBETH	Not yet.
MACDUFF	He did command me to call timely on him: I have almost slipp'd the hour.
MACBETH	I'll bring you to him.
MACDUFF	I know this is a joyful trouble to you; 45 But yet 'tis one.
MACBETH	The labour we delight in physics pain. This is the door.
MACDUFF	I'll make so bold to call, For 'tis my limited service. *[Exit]*
LENNOX	Goes the king hence to-day?
MACBETH	He does: he did appoint so. 50
LENNOX	The night has been unruly: where we lay, Our chimneys were blown down; and, as they say, Lamentings heard i' the air; strange screams of death, And prophesying with accents terrible Of dire combustion and confus'd events 55 New hatch'd to the woeful time. The obscure bird Clamour'd the livelong night; some say the earth Was feverous and did shake.
MACBETH	'Twas a rough night.
LENNOX	My young remembrance cannot parallel A fellow to it. 60 *[Re-enter MACDUFF]*
MACDUFF	O horror! horror! horror! Tongue nor heart Cannot conceive nor name thee!

ORIGINAL

PORTER	You're right, but I overcame the consequences of drunkenness.
MACDUFF	Is Macbeth awake? *[Enter MACBETH]* We woke him up with our knocking. Here he comes.
LENNOX	Good morning, sir.
MACBETH	Good morning to you both.
MACDUFF	Is the king awake, noble lord?
MACBETH	Not yet.
MACDUFF	He asked me to call for him on time. I'm almost late.
MACBETH	I'll take you to him.
MACDUFF	I know this is not a real bother for you, but it is an inconvenience.
MACBETH	Running the errand takes away the bother. This is Duncan's door.
MACDUFF	I will knock boldly because that is my job. *[He goes out]*
LENNOX	Is the king traveling today?
MACBETH	Yes. He made arrangements to leave.
LENNOX	It was a bad night. At our stop, the wind blew down chimneys. People claimed to have heard moaning and death cries and frightful prophecies of fire and social turmoil. The night bird fretted all night; some people heard earth tremors.
MACBETH	It was a windy night.
LENNOX	In all my years, I can't remember so bad a night. *[Re-enter MACDUFF]*
MACDUFF	O horror! horror! horror! Neither words nor emotions can believe it or call its name.

ACT II

TRANSLATION

MACBETH AND LENNOX	What's the matter?

MACDUFF   Confusion now hath made his masterpiece!
Most sacrilegious murder hath broke ope
The Lord's anointed temple, and stole thence   65
The life o' the building!

MACBETH   What is 't you say? the life?

LENNOX   Mean you his majesty?

MACDUFF   Approach the chamber, and destroy your sight
With a new Gorgon: do not bid me speak;   70
See, and then speak yourselves.
[Exeunt MACBETH and LENNOX]
                                        Awake! awake!
Ring the alarum-bell. Murder and treason!
Banquo and Donalbain! Malcolm! awake!
Shake off this downy sleep, death's counterfeit,
And look on death itself! up, up, and see   75
The great doom's image! Malcolm! Banquo!
As from your graves rise up, and walk like sprites,
To countenance this horror! Ring the bell.
[Bell rings. Enter LADY MACBETH]

LADY MACBETH   What's the business,
That such a hideous trumpet calls to parley   80
The sleepers of the house? speak, speak!

MACDUFF   O gentle lady!
'Tis not for you to hear what I can speak;
The repetition in a woman's ear
Would murder as it fell.
[Enter BANQUO]
                            O Banquo! Banquo!
Our royal master's murder'd!

LADY MACBETH   Woe, alas!   85
What! in our house?

BANQUO   Too cruel any where.
Dear Duff, I prithee, contradict thyself,
And say it is not so.
[Re-enter MACBETH and LENNOX]

ORIGINAL

MACBETH AND LENNOX	What's happened?
MACDUFF	The worst kind of destruction. A sinful murderer has stabbed the king, whom God chose to rule Scotland.
MACBETH	What are you saying? He's dead?
LENNOX	Do you mean the king?
MACDUFF	Look in the bedroom and see the terrible monstrosity. Don't ask me to tell you. Look for yourselves and tell me what you see. *[MACBETH and LENNOX depart]* Wake the household! Ring the alarm. Murder and treason! Banquo and Donalbain! Malcolm! wake up! Open your eyes and see the king's eyes closed forever. Malcolm! Banquo! Rise like dead men from the grave and look on this terrible assassination. Ring the alarm. *[Bell rings. Enter LADY MACBETH]*
LADY MACBETH	What's the cause of this uproar in a sleeping household? Tell me!
MACDUFF	O gentle lady! It is too terrible to say to a woman. The news might kill you. *[Enter BANQUO]* Oh Banquo! Banquo! Our king has been murdered!
LADY MACBETH	Oh, no! A murder in our house?
BANQUO	This murder should not have happened in any house. Duff, please, say it isn't so. *[Re-enter MACBETH and LENNOX]*

ACT II

TRANSLATION

MACBETH	Had I but died an hour before this chance
	I had liv'd a blessed time; for, from this instant, 90
	There's nothing serious in mortality.
	All is but toys; renown and grace is dead,
	The wine of life is drawn, and the mere lees
	Is left this vault to brag of.
	[Enter MALCOLM and DONALBAIN]

DONALBAIN   What is amiss?

MACBETH   You are, and do not know 't: 95
The spring, the head, the fountain of your blood
Is stopp'd; the very source of it is stopp'd.

MACDUFF   Your royal father's murder'd.

MALCOLM   O! by whom?

LENNOX   Those of his chamber, as it seem'd, had done 't:
Their hands and faces were all badg'd with blood;   100
So were their daggers, which unwip'd we found
Upon their pillows: they star'd, and were distracted;
no man's life
was to be trusted with them.

MACBETH   O! yet I do repent me of my fury.
That I did kill them.

MACDUFF   Wherefore did you so?   105

MACBETH   Who can be wise, amaz'd, temperate and furious,
Loyal and neutral, in a moment? No man:
The expedition of my violent love
Outran the pauser, reason. Here lay Duncan,
His silver skin lac'd with his golden blood;   110
And his gash'd stabs look'd like a breach in nature
For ruin's wasteful entrance: there, the murderers,
Steep'd in the colours of their trade, their daggers
Unmannerly breech'd with gore: who could refrain,
That had a heart to love, and in that heart   115
Courage to make's love known?

LADY MACBETH   Help me hence, ho!

MACDUFF   Look to the lady.

MALCOLM   *[Aside to DONALBAIN]*   Why do we hold our tongues,
That most may claim this argument for ours?

MACBETH	If I had died an hour ago, I would be better off. From this time on, there is nothing worth living for. *[Enter MALCOLM and DONALBAIN]*
DONALBAIN	What is wrong?
MACBETH	You royal princes have lost the head of the family.
MACDUFF	The king has been murdered.
MALCOLM	Who did it?
LENNOX	His servants appear to be guilty. There is bloody evidence on their hands and faces as well as their daggers, which they left unwiped on their pillows. They gaped and muttered; they could never be trusted again.
MACBETH	I regret that, in my rage, I killed them.
MACDUFF	Why did you do that?
MACBETH	Could anybody be logical and terrified, composed and enraged, loyal to the king and fair to the suspects at the same time? No. Before I could think sensibly, I struck them out of love for the king. In front of me was Duncan, his royal skin coated in blood; the stab wounds looked like a violation of his body. There lay the killers soaked in blood, their daggers drenched in gore. Who could overcome love for the king and not want to slay his killers?
LADY MACBETH	I feel faint. Help me!
MACDUFF	Look after the lady.
MALCOLM	*[Aside to DONALBAIN]* Why are we silent when we should be stating our outrage?

ACT II

TRANSLATION

DONALBAIN	*[Aside to MALCOLM]* What should be spoken
	Here where our fate, hid in an auger-hole, 120
	May rush and seize us? Let's away: our tears
	Are not yet brew'd.

MALCOLM	*[Aside to DONALBAIN]* Nor our strong sorrow
	Upon the foot of motion.

BANQUO   Look to the lady:
[LADY MACBETH is carried out]
And when we have our naked frailties hid,   125
That suffer in exposure, let us meet,
And question this most bloody piece of work,
To know it further. Fears and scruples shake us:
In the great hand of God I stand, and thence
Against the undivulg'd pretence I fight   130
Of treasonous malice.

MACDUFF   And so do I.

ALL   So all.

MACBETH   Let's briefly put on manly readiness,
And meet i' the hall together.

ALL   Well contented.
[Exeunt all but MALCOLM and DONALBAIN]

MALCOLM   What will you do? Let's not consort with them:
To show an unfelt sorrow is an office   135
Which the false man does easy. I'll to England.

DONALBAIN   To Ireland, I; our separated fortune
Shall keep us both the safer: where we are,
There's daggers in men's smiles: the near in blood,
The nearer bloody.

MALCOLM   This murderous shaft that's shot   140
Hath not yet lighted, and our safest way
Is to avoid the aim: therefore, to horse;
And let us not be dainty of leave-taking,
But shift away: there's warrant in that theft
Which steals itself when there's no mercy left.   145
[Exeunt]

DONALBAIN	*[Aside to MALCOLM]* What can we say when we may suffer the same fate? Let's escape. Our grief is still to come.
MALCOLM	*[Aside to DONALBAIN]* We are not ready to express our sorrow.
BANQUO	Take care of the lady. *[LADY MACBETH is carried out]* When we are calmer, let's meet to investigate this killing. Fear and suspicion unnerve us. I leave to God the meantime until I can face this treasonous act.

ACT II

MACDUFF	I agree.
ALL	We all do.
MACBETH	Let's quiet our nerves and meet in the hall.
ALL	That's a good idea. *[All leave except MALCOLM and DONALBAIN]*
MALCOLM	What are you going to do? Let's not discuss the crime with the others. It is easy for the killer to pretend sorrow. I'm leaving for England.
DONALBAIN	I'm going to Ireland. If we separate, we shall be safer. Where both heirs to the throne remain, they make an easy target for more assassinations.
MALCOLM	This plot is not finished. It is safest for us to avoid being the next target. Let's mount our horses and ride heartily away. We are right to sneak away from this crime-ridden castle. *[They depart]*

TRANSLATION

ACT II, SCENE 4

The same. Without the castle.

[Enter Ross and an OLD MAN]

OLD MAN　　　Threescore and ten I can remember well;
Within the volume of which time I have seen
Hours dreadful and things strange, but this sore night
Hath trifled former knowings.

ROSS　　　　　　　　　　　Ah! good father,
Thou seest, the heavens, as troubled with man's act,　　5
Threaten his bloody stage: by the clock 'tis day,
And yet dark night strangles the travelling lamp.
Is 't night's predominance, or the day's shame,
That darkness does the face of earth entomb,
When living light should kiss it?

OLD MAN　　　　　　　　　　　'Tis unnatural,　　10
Even like the deed that's done. On Tuesday last,
A falcon, towering in her pride of place,
Was by a mousing owl hawk'd at and kill'd.

ROSS　　　And Duncan's horses—a thing most strange and certain—
Beauteous and swift, the minions of their race,　　15
Turn'd wild in nature, broke their stalls, flung out,
Contending 'gainst obedience, as they would
Make war with mankind.

OLD MAN　　　　　　　　'Tis said they eat each other.

ROSS　　　They did so, to the amazement of mine eyes,
That look'd upon 't. Here comes the good Macduff.　　20
[Enter MACDUFF]
How goes the world, sir, now?

MACDUFF　　　　　　　　　　Why, see you not?

ROSS　　　Is 't known who did this more than bloody deed?

MACDUFF　　　Those that Macbeth hath slain.

ROSS　　　　　　　　　　　Alas, the day!
What good could they pretend?

MACDUFF　　　　　　　　　　They were suborn'd.
Malcolm and Donalbain, the king's two sons,　　25
Are stol'n away and fled, which put upon them
Suspicion of the deed.

ORIGINAL

ACT II, SCENE 4

The same. Without the castle.

[Enter Ross and an OLD MAN]

OLD MAN   I am over 70 years old and have never seen so dreadful a time as this.

ROSS   Old man, you see heaven in turmoil over earthly crimes. The clock says it is daytime, but dark crimes hinder the light. Is it the power of evil or the shame of goodness that makes the day seem so dark?

OLD MAN   The day is as unthinkable as the crime. Last Tuesday, an owl killed a falcon in her roost.

ROSS   It is odd that Duncan's beautiful, fast horses went wild, broke out of the stalls, and refused to be controlled.

OLD MAN   It is rumored that they bit each other.

ROSS   They did. Everyone in the stable was amazed. Here comes Macduff. *[Enter MACDUFF]* Are things settling down?

MACDUFF   Don't you see?

ROSS   Did you learn who assassinated the king?

MACDUFF   The servants whom Macbeth killed.

ROSS   What good would they gain from killing the king?

MACDUFF   Someone hired them. Malcolm and Donalbain, the king's sons, have sneaked away. Their departure makes them seem guilty.

ROSS	'Gainst nature still!
	Thriftless ambition, that wilt ravin up
	Thine own life's means! Then 'tis most like
	The sovereignty will fall upon Macbeth. 30
MACDUFF	He is already nam'd, and gone to Scone
	To be invested.
ROSS	Where is Duncan's body?
MACDUFF	Carried to Colmekill,
	The sacred storehouse of his predecessors
	And guardian of their bones.
ROSS	Will you to Scone? 35
MACDUFF	No cousin, I'll to Fife.
ROSS	Well, I will thither.
MACDUFF	Well, may you see things well done there: adieu!
	Lest our old robes sit easier than our new!
ROSS	Farewell, father.
OLD MAN	God's benison go with you: and with those 40
	That would make good of bad, and friends of foes!
	[Exeunt]

ORIGINAL

ROSS	This is strange business that will destroy the princes' chances of success. It is likely that Macbeth will succeed Duncan as king.
MACDUFF	Macbeth is already named the successor. He has gone to Scone, the scene of royal crownings, to receive the title.
ROSS	Where is Duncan's body?
MACDUFF	Conveyed to the island of Iona in the west, the burial place of Scots royalty.
ROSS	Are you going to the crowning at Scone?
MACDUFF	No, friend, I'm going home to Fife.
ROSS	Well, I will go to Scone.
MACDUFF	I hope you see the ceremony properly performed. Goodbye. I fear that the future will not be so contented as the past.
ROSS	Goodbye.
OLD MAN	God's blessing on you and with those who are trying to settle unrest in Scotland and solve this crime. *[They depart]*

ACT II

TRANSLATION

ACT III, SCENE 1

Forres. A room in the palace.

[Enter BANQUO]

BANQUO   Thou hast it now: King, Cawdor, Glamis, all,
As the weird women promis'd; and, I fear,
Thou play'dst most foully for 't; yet it was said
It should not stand in thy posterity,
But that myself should be the root and father   5
Of many kings. If there come truth from them,—
As upon thee, Macbeth, their speeches shine,—
Why, by the verities on thee made good,
May they not be my oracles as well,
And set me up in hope? But, hush! no more.   10
*[Sennet sounded. Enter MACBETH, as king; LADY
MACBETH, as queen; LENNOX, ROSS, Lords, Ladies,
and Attendants]*

MACBETH   Here's our chief guest.

LADY MACBETH   If he had been forgotten,
It had been as a gap in our great feast,
And all-thing unbecoming.

MACBETH   To-night we hold a solemn supper, sir,
And I'll request your presence.

BANQUO   Let your highness   15
Command upon me; to the which my duties
Are with a most indissoluble tie
For ever knit.

MACBETH   Ride you this afternoon?

ACT III, SCENE 1

Forres, an ancient capital city in northern Scotland on the Moray coast. A room in the royal palace.

[Enter BANQUO]

BANQUO	You have it all—king, Lord of Cawdor, Lord of Glamis, all, just as the witches promised. I fear that you advanced through criminal methods. But the witches said that you would not create a dynasty. I will be the source and father of a royal line. If their predictions come true as they have for you, will they not also give me hope of advancement? But, silence, don't think any more of it. *[A fanfare announces the arrival of royalty. Enter MACBETH, as king; LADY MACBETH, as queen; LENNOX, ROSS, Lords, Ladies, and Attendants]*
MACBETH	Here's our main guest.
LADY MACBETH	If we had left him out, we would have ruined our feast by such an oversight.
MACBETH	We are holding a state dinner, sir. I want you to attend.
BANQUO	If the king commands me, it is my duty to obey.
MACBETH	Are you going riding this afternoon?

ACT III

TRANSLATION

BANQUO	Ay, my good lord.

MACBETH   We should have else desir'd your good advice—   20
Which still hath been both grave and prosperous —
In this day's council; but we'll take to-morrow.
Is 't far you ride?

BANQUO   As far, my lord, as will fill up the time
'Twixt this and supper; go not my horse the better,   25
I must become a borrower of the night
For a dark hour or twain.

MACBETH   Fail not our feast.

BANQUO   My lord, I will not.

MACBETH   We hear our bloody cousins are bestow'd
In England and in Ireland, not confessing   30
Their cruel parricide, filling their hearers
With strange invention; but of that to-morrow,
When therewithal we shall have cause of state
Craving us jointly. Hie you to horse; adieu
Till you return at night. Goes Fleance with you?   35

BANQUO   Ay, my good lord; our time does call upon 's.

MACBETH   I wish your horses swift and sure of foot;
And so I do commend you to their backs.
Farewell. *[Exit BANQUO]*
Let every man be master of his time   40
Till seven at night; to make society
The sweeter welcome, we will keep ourself
Till supper-time alone; while then, God be with you!
[Exeunt all but MACBETH and an Attendant]
Sirrah, a word with you. Attend those men
Our pleasure?

BANQUO	Yes, my lord.
MACBETH	For today's council session, I wanted your advice, which has always been serious and beneficial, but I'll wait for it until tomorrow. Are you riding far?
BANQUO	As far as I can before dinner. If my horse is not fast, I may be out an hour or two after dark.
MACBETH	Don't forget the state dinner.
BANQUO	My lord, I will be there.
MACBETH	I have heard that Malcolm and Donalbain have fled to England and Ireland, but do not confess their part in the assassination plot. They are telling other people wild stories. We'll discuss them tomorrow when we can confer together. Off with you to your ride. Goodbye until you return tonight. Is your son Fleance riding with you?
BANQUO	Yes, my lord. We have arranged to leave at this time.
MACBETH	I hope your horses are swift and sure-footed. Have a good ride. Goodbye. *[BANQUO goes out]* Let everyone have free time until 7:00 p.m. to make our meeting that much more enjoyable. I will be alone until dinner. Until then, God be with you! *[They all depart except MACBETH and his servant]* Sir, may I have a word with you. Did you state my command to those men?

ACT III

TRANSLATION

ATTENDANT	They are, my lord, without the palace gate. 45
MACBETH	Bring them before us. *[Exit Attendant]*
	To be thus is nothing;
	But to be safely thus. Our fears in Banquo
	Stick deep, and in his royalty of nature
	Reigns that which would be fear'd: 'tis much he dares, 50
	And, to that dauntless temper of his mind,
	He hath a wisdom that doth guide his valour
	To act in safety. There is none but he
	Whose being I do fear; and under him
	My genius is rebuk'd, as it is said 55
	Mark Antony's was by Caesar. He chid the sisters
	When first they put the name of king upon me,
	And bade them speak to him; then, prophet-like,
	They hail'd him father to a line of kings.
	Upon my head they plac'd a fruitless crown, 60
	And put a barren sceptre in my gripe,
	Thence to be wrench'd with an unlineal hand,
	No son of mine succeeding. If 't be so,
	For Banquo's issue have I fil'd my mind;
	For them the gracious Duncan have I murder'd; 65
	Put rancours in the vessel of my peace
	Only for them; and mine eternal jewel
	Given to the common enemy of man,
	To make them kings, the seed of Banquo kings!
	Rather than so, come fate into the list, 70
	And champion me to the utterance! Who's there?
	[Re-enter Attendant, with two Murderers]
	Now go to the door, and stay there till we call.
	[Exit Attendant]
	Was it not yesterday we spoke together?
FIRST MURDERER	It was, so please your highness.
MACBETH	Well then, now
	Have you consider'd of my speeches? Know 75
	That it was he in the times past which held you
	So under fortune, which you thought had been
	Our innocent self. This I made good to you
	In our last conference, pass'd in probation with you,
	How you were borne in hand, how cross'd, the instruments, 80
	Who wrought with them, and all things else that might
	To half a soul and to a notion craz'd
	Say, 'Thus did Banquo.'

ATTENDANT	My lord, they are waiting outside the palace gate.
MACBETH	Bring them to me. *[The servant goes out]* To be king is not as important as to be secure on the throne. My fear of Banquo troubles me. In his character is a royal nature that frightens me. He is ambitious, but self-controlled. He is wise enough to behave sensibly. He is the only person I fear. He scolds my spirit the way that Julius Caesar rebuked Mark Antony. He scolded the witches when they prophesied that I would be king. He asked they prophesy for him. Like seers, they called him the father of a royal dynasty. In my hand, the witches placed a short-term advancement to the throne. My scepter will not pass to my son. If this prophecy is true, I have assassinated Duncan to make way for Banquo's children to become kings. This prophecy gives me no peace. My crowning was the devil's work. I will only make Banquo's sons kings! I welcome fate to settle the competition between me and Banquo! Who is approaching? *[Re-enter servant, with two Murderers]* Remain at the door until I call you. *[The servant leaves]* Didn't we talk yesterday?

ACT III

FIRST MURDERER	Yes, sir, we did.
MACBETH	Since then, have you considered my words? It was Banquo who, in the past, wronged you. You blamed me. I explained to you at our last meeting and gave you proof how you were mistreated and double-crossed. The documents prove that Banquo is your enemy.

FIRST MURDERER	You made it known to us.
MACBETH	I did so; and went further, which is now
	Our point of second meeting. Do you find 85
	Your patience so predominant in your nature
	That you can let this go? Are you so gospell'd
	To pray for this good man and for his issue,
	Whose heavy hand hath bow'd you to the grave
	And beggar'd yours for ever?
FIRST MURDERER	We are men, my liege. 90
MACBETH	Ay, in the catalogue ye go for men;
	As hounds and greyhounds, mongrels, spaniels, curs,
	Shoughs, water-rugs, and demi-wolves, are clept
	All by the name of dogs; the valu'd file
	Distinguishes the swift, the slow the subtle, 95
	The housekeeper, the hunter, every one
	According to the gift which bounteous nature
	Hath in him clos'd; whereby he does receive
	Particular addition, from the bill
	That writes them all alike: and so of men. 100
	Now, if you have a station in the file,
	Not i' the worst rank of manhood, say it;
	And I will put that business in your bosoms,
	Whose execution takes your enemy off,
	Grapples you to the heart and love of us, 105
	Who wear our health but sickly in his life,
	Which in his death were perfect.
SECOND MURDERER	I am one, my liege,
	Whom the vile blows and buffets of the world
	Have so incens'd that I am reckless what
	I do to spite the world.
FIRST MURDERER	And I another, 110
	So weary with disasters, tugg'd with fortune,
	That I would set my life on any chance,
	To mend it or be rid on 't.
MACBETH	Both of you
	Know Banquo was your enemy.
SECOND MURDERER	True, my lord.

FIRST MURDERER	You made it clear.
MACBETH	Yes, I did and I also explained the purpose of our second meeting. Are you willing to allow Banquo to continue wronging you? Are you so religious that you can pray for this man and his children even though he has burdened and robbed you?
FIRST MURDERER	We are normal men, my king.
MACBETH	Yes, you are listed like men like breeds of hounds, runners, mutts, spaniels, curs, shaggy dogs, swimmers, and dogs that are part wolves. All appear under the heading of "dogs." An evaluation of each dog identifies the fast runner, the slow, the sneaky, the housedog, the hunting dog, each according to its inborn traits. By this cataloguing of dogs, individual types appear alongside their qualities. It is the same with people. If you have a quality that raises you above the lowest of humanity, then say so. I will assign you tasks that will rid you of an enemy who does not honor the king. This enemy's death will perfect my rule.
SECOND MURDERER	I am the kind of man, my king, who grows enraged by hard times. I become reckless to avenge myself on the world.
FIRST MURDERER	I, too, am tired of disaster and bad luck. I want to seize the opportunity to improve my fortune or cancel it.
MACBETH	Both of you know that Banquo is the cause of your misfortune.
SECOND MURDERER	That's true, my lord.

ACT III

TRANSLATION

MACBETH	So is he mine; and in such bloody distance 115
	That every minute of his being thrusts
	Against my near'st of life: and though I could
	With bare-fac'd power sweep him from my sight
	And bid my will avouch it, yet I must not,
	For certain friends that are both his and mine, 120
	Whose loves I may not drop, but wail his fall
	Whom I myself struck down; and thence it is
	That I to your assistance do make love,
	Masking the business from the common eye
	For sundry weighty reasons.

SECOND   We shall, my lord,   125
MURDERER   Perform what you command us.

FIRST   Though our lives—
MURDERER

MACBETH	Your spirits shine through you. Within this hour at most
	I will advise you where to plant yourselves,
	Acquaint you with the perfect spy o' the time,
	The moment on 't; for 't must be done to-night, 130
	And something from the palace; always thought
	That I require a clearness: and with him—
	To leave no rubs nor botches in the work—
	Fleance his son, that keeps him company,
	Whose absence is no less material to me 135
	Than is his father's, must embrace the fate
	Of that dark hour. Resolve yourselves apart;
	I'll come to you anon.

SECOND   We are resolv'd, my lord.
MURDERER

MACBETH   I'll call upon you straight: abide within.
                            [Exeunt Murderers]
          It is concluded: Banquo, thy soul's flight,   140
          If it find heaven, must find it out to-night. *[Exit]*

MACBETH	Banquo is also my enemy. Every minute that he lives, he threatens my life. Although I could overcome him, I must not for political reasons. Mutual friends of mine and of Banquo would blame me for killing him. To end his conniving, I need your help in murdering him out of sight of my court.
SECOND MURDERER	We will do what you command, my lord.
FIRST MURDERER	Even if the task kills us.
MACBETH	I see your character in your actions. In an hour, I will inform you where to wait for Banquo and when to kill him. It must be done tonight away from the palace. I don't want to fall under suspicion. To rid me of this enemy, you must also kill Fleance, his son and companion, who is as dangerous to me as is Banquo. Make up your minds in private. I'll return to you soon.
SECOND MURDERER	We are already determined, my lord.
MACBETH	I will summon you directly. Stay inside. *[The Murderers go out]* It is finished. Banquo, if you ever get to heaven, it will be tonight. *[MACBETH goes out]*

ACT III

ACT III, SCENE 2

The same. Another room in the palace.

[Enter LADY MACBETH and a Servant]

LADY MACBETH   Is Banquo gone from court?

SERVANT   Ay, madam, but returns again to-night.

LADY MACBETH   Say to the king, I would attend his leisure
For a few words.

SERVANT   Madam, I will. *[Exit]*

LADY MACBETH   Nought's had, all's spent,
Where our desire is got without content: 5
'Tis safer to be that which we destroy
Than by destruction dwell in doubtful joy.
[Enter MACBETH]
How now, my lord! why do you keep alone,
Of sorriest fancies your companions making,
Using those thoughts which should indeed have died   10
With them they think on? Things without all remedy
Should be without regard: what's done is done.

MACBETH   We have scotch'd the snake, not kill'd it:
She'll close and be herself, whilst our poor malice
Remains in danger of her former tooth.   15
But let the frame of things disjoint, both the worlds suffer,
Ere we will eat our meal in fear, and sleep
In the affliction of these terrible dreams
That shake us nightly. Better be with the dead,
Whom we, to gain our peace, have sent to peace,   20
Than on the torture of the mind to lie
In restless ecstacy. Duncan is in his grave;
After life's fitful fever he sleeps well;
Treason has done his worst: nor steel, nor poison,
Malice domestic, foreign levy, nothing   25
Can touch him further.

LADY MACBETH   Come on;
Gentle my lord, sleek o'er your rugged looks;
Be bright and jovial among your guests to-night.

ORIGINAL

ACT III, SCENE 2

The same. Another room in the palace.

[Enter LADY MACBETH and a Servant]

LADY MACBETH Is Banquo away from the palace?

SERVANT Yes, ma'am, but he will return tonight.

LADY MACBETH Tell the king I want to talk to him.

SERVANT Yes, ma'am. *[He departs]*

LADY MACBETH We have gained nothing. We wasted our energies when we seized the throne without securing it. It's better to be a dead monarch than to live in doubt. *[Enter MACBETH]* Why do you prefer solitude, my lord, where regretful imaginings burden you and destroy your concentration? What you can't change you shouldn't worry about. What's done is done.

MACBETH We have wounded the snake, not killed it. It will heal and endanger us once more with its fangs. Let the world fall apart rather than we continue living in fear and sleeping through terrible dreams every night. We might as well be dead like Duncan than to live on with tortured minds. Duncan is buried and at peace. He can suffer no more from traitors, daggers, poison, evil Scots, foreign armies. Nothing can harm him.

LADY MACBETH Please, my sweet lord, relax your face. Be a jolly, happy host tonight to your guests.

ACT III

TRANSLATION

MACBETH	So shall I, love; and so, I pray, be you.
	Let your remembrance apply to Banquo; 30
	Present him eminence, both with eye and tongue:
	Unsafe the while, that we
	Must lave our honours in these flattering streams,
	And make our faces vizards to our hearts,
	Disguising what they are.
LADY MACBETH	You must leave this. 35
MACBETH	O! full of scorpions is my mind, dear wife;
	Thou know'st that Banquo and his Fleance lives.
LADY MACBETH	But in them nature's copy's not eterne.
MACBETH	There's comfort yet; they are assailable;
	Then be thou jocund. Ere the bat hath flown 40
	His cloister'd flight, ere to black Hecate's summons
	The shard-born beetle with his drowsy hums
	Hath rung night's yawning peal, there shall be done
	A deed of dreadful note.
LADY MACBETH	What's to be done?
MACBETH	Be innocent of the knowledge, dearest chuck 45
	Till thou applaud the deed. Come, seeling night,
	Scarf up the tender eye of pitiful day,
	And with thy bloody and invisible hand
	Cancel and tear to pieces that great bond
	Which keeps me pale! Light thickens, and the crow 50
	Makes wing to the rooky wood;
	Good things of day begin to droop and drowse,
	Whiles night's black agents to their preys do rouse.
	Thou marvell'st at my words: but hold thee still;
	Things bad begun make strong themselves by ill: 55
	So, prithee, go with me. *[Exeunt]*

MACBETH	I will, my love. You, too, must be hospitable. Remember Banquo and treat him with worthy looks and words. It is dangerous to speak of honor and wear false faces when our hearts are dishonorable.
LADY MACBETH	You must stop moping.
MACBETH	My mind is filled with scorpions, dear wife. I can't relax while Banquo and Fleance survive.
LADY MACBETH	They can't live forever.
MACBETH	That's true. They are vulnerable. Then be happy. Before the bat flies from his hiding place; before the hard-shelled beetle answers the witch-goddess's call, there will be a terrible calamity.
LADY MACBETH	What are you planning?
MACBETH	Keep your innocence, sweetheart, until you learn of my plot. Come, darkness, and conceal daylight. Then the invisible assassins can destroy the one hindrance to my contentment. Evening is falling. Crows are flying back to the woods. Day departs. By night, the murderers can attack their victims. You look astonished, but don't question me. I can correct a bad beginning with one more crime. Please, go with me. *[They depart]*

ACT III

TRANSLATION

ACT III, SCENE 3

The same. A park with a road leading to the palace.

[Enter three Murderers]

FIRST MURDERER   But who did bid thee join with us?

THIRD MURDERER   Macbeth.

SECOND MURDERER   He needs not our mistrust, since he delivers
Our offices and what we have to do
To the direction just.

FIRST MURDERER   Then stand with us.
The west yet glimmers with some streaks of day: 5
Now spurs the lated traveller apace
To gain the timely inn; and near approaches
The subject of our watch.

THIRD MURDERER   Hark! I hear horses.

BANQUO   *[Within]* Give us a light there, ho!

SECOND MURDERER   Then 'tis he: the rest
That are within the note of expectation   10
Already are i' the court.

FIRST MURDERER   His horses go about.

THIRD MURDERER   Almost a mile; but he does usually,
So all men do, from hence to the palace gate
Make it their walk.
[Enter BANQUO and FLEANCE, with a torch]

SECOND MURDERER   A light, a light!

THIRD MURDERER   'Tis he.

FIRST MURDERER   Stand to 't.   15

BANQUO   It will be rain to-night.

ACT III, SCENE 3

The same. A park with a road leading to the palace.

[Enter three Murderers]

FIRST MURDERER	Who sent you to join us two?
THIRD MURDERER	Macbeth sent me.
SECOND MURDERER	He can trust us, since he has given us explicit instructions.
FIRST MURDERER	Stay here. It is nearly dark. Our victim is approaching.
THIRD MURDERER	Listen. I hear horses.
BANQUO	*[Within]* Servant, light the path.
SECOND MURDERER	It's Banquo. All the other guests are at the palace.
FIRST MURDERER	His horses move to the rear of the castle.
THIRD MURDERER	It is a mile away. Like most visitors, he plans to walk the rest of the way to the front gate. *[Enter BANQUO and FLEANCE, with a torch]*
SECOND MURDERER	Hold up a light!
THIRD MURDERER	It's Banquo.
FIRST MURDERER	Let's attack.
BANQUO	It is going to rain tonight.

ACT III

TRANSLATION

FIRST MURDERER	Let it come down. *[They set upon BANQUO]*
BANQUO	O, treachery! Fly, good Fleance, fly, fly, fly! Thou mayst revenge. O slave! *[Dies. FLEANCE escapes]*
THIRD MURDERER	Who did strike out the light?
FIRST MURDERER	Was 't not the way?
THIRD MURDERER	There's but one down; the son is fled.
SECOND MURDERER	We have lost 20 Best half of our affair.
FIRST MURDERER	Well, let's away, and say how much is done. *[Exeunt]*

FIRST MURDERER	Let it fall. *[They attack BANQUO]*
BANQUO	Oh, an ambush! Run, Fleance, run! You may avenge my death. Oh, villain! *[BANQUO dies. FLEANCE escapes]*
THIRD MURDERER	Who ignited the light?
FIRST MURDERER	Didn't we succeed?
THIRD MURDERER	We killed Banquo; Fleance escaped.
SECOND MURDERER	We finished only half our job.
FIRST MURDERER	Well, let's go back to the king and report one murder. *[They depart]*

TRANSLATION

ACT III, SCENE 4

The same. A room of state in the palace.

[A Banquet prepared. Enter MACBETH, LADY MACBETH, ROSS, LENNOX, Lords, and Attendants]

MACBETH	You know your own degrees; sit down: at first and last,
	The hearty welcome.
LORDS	Thanks to your majesty.
MACBETH	Ourself will mingle with society
	And play the humble host.
	Our hostess keeps her state, but in best time 5
	We will require her welcome.
LADY MACBETH	Pronounce it for me, sir, to all our friends;
	For my heart speaks they are welcome.
	[Enter First Murderer, to the door]
MACBETH	See, they encounter thee with their hearts' thanks;
	Both sides are even: here I'll sit i' the midst: 10
	Be large in mirth; anon, we'll drink a measure
	The table round. *[Approaching the door]* There's
	blood upon thy face.
MURDERER	'Tis Banquo's, then.
MACBETH	'Tis better thee without than he within.
	Is he dispatch'd? 15
MURDERER	My lord, his throat is cut; that I did for him.
MACBETH	Thou art the best o' the cut-throats; yet he's good
	That did the like for Fleance: if thou didst it,
	Thou art the nonpareil.
MURDERER	Most royal sir,
	Fleance is 'scap'd. 20
MACBETH	Then comes my fit again: I had else been perfect;
	Whole as the marble, founded as the rock,
	As broad and general as the casing air:
	But now I am cabin'd, cribb'd, confined, bound in
	To saucy doubts and fears. But Banquo's safe? 25
MURDERER	Ay, my good lord; safe in a ditch he bides,
	With twenty trenched gashes on his head,
	The least a death to nature.

ACT III, SCENE 4

The same. A room of state in the palace.

[A Banquet is served. Enter MACBETH, LADY MACBETH, ROSS, LENNOX, Lords, and Attendants]

MACBETH You know the proper seating arrangement. Sit down by rank. Welcome to all, first and last.

LORDS Thank you, your majesty.

MACBETH I will mingle with the guests and be a humble host. The queen prefers to sit at her place. Later, I will ask her to help me welcome guests.

LADY MACBETH Speak for me, sir, to all our friends. My heart is full of welcome to them. *[Enter First Murderer, to the door]*

MACBETH See how they view you with genuine thanks. I will sit in the middle of the table. Be jolly. Soon, we will pass drinks to all guests. *[Approaching the door]* Your face is bloody.

MURDERER It is Banquo's blood.

MACBETH I would rather have his blood on your face than in his body. Is he dead?

MURDERER My lord, I slit his throat.

MACBETH You are the best of assassins. I will thank the assassin who slew Fleance. If you did it, you are without equal.

MURDERER My king, Fleance escaped.

MACBETH My terror returns. I wanted everything perfect, like unflawed marble, like a rock sitting upon earth. But I feel cramped, closeted, confined, bound by doubt and fear. Did you really kill Banquo?

MURDERER Yes, my lord. He lies in a ditch with twenty gashes on his head, any one of which might have killed him.

ACT III

TRANSLATION

MACBETH   Thanks for that.
There the grown serpent lies: the worm that's fled
Hath nature that in time will venom breed,   30
No teeth for the present. Get thee gone; to-morrow
We'll hear ourselves again. *[Exit Murderer]*

LADY MACBETH   My royal lord,
You do not give the cheer: the feast is sold
That is not often vouch'd, while 'tis a-making,
'Tis given with welcome: to feed were best at home;   35
From thence, the sauce to meat is ceremony;
Meeting were bare without it.

MACBETH   Sweet remembrancer!
Now good digestion wait on appetite,
And health on both!

LENNOX   May it please your highness sit?
*[The Ghost of BANQUO enters, and
sits in MACBETH'S place]*

MACBETH   Here had we now our country's honour roof'd,   40
Were the grac'd person of our Banquo present;
Who may I rather challenge for unkindness
Than pity for mischance!

ROSS   His absence, sir,
Lays blame upon his promise. Please 't your highness
To grace us with your royal company.   45

MACBETH   The table's full.

LENNOX   Here is a place reserv'd, sir.

MACBETH   Where?

LENNOX   Here, my good lord. What is 't that moves your highness?

MACBETH   Which of you have done this?

LORDS   What, my good lord?

MACBETH   Thou canst not say I did it: never shake   50
Thy gory locks at me.

ROSS   Gentlemen, rise; his highness is not well.

LADY MACBETH Sit, worthy friends: my lord is often thus,
And hath been from his youth: pray you, keep seat;
The fit is momentary; upon a thought   55
He will again be well. If much you note him,
You shall offend him and extend his passion:
Feed, and regard him not. Are you a man?

MACBETH	Thanks for the one murder. But a dead parent does not stop his child from plotting treachery. Go. Tomorrow, we will discuss the matter again. *[The Murderer departs]*
LADY MACBETH	My king, you are not cheerful. Unless you welcome the guests, they will feel that they are paying for their dinner. It would be better to eat at home. Eating at the palace is unsatisfying if you do not act the part of host.
MACBETH	A sweet reminder! Digestion requires hunger. Health requires both.
LENNOX	Would you take a seat, sir? *[The Ghost of BANQUO enters, and sits in MACBETH'S place]*
MACBETH	I could enjoy my honors if Banquo were here tonight. I hope he is only absent, not fallen on bad luck.
ROSS	His absence, sir, speaks ill of him. Please, your highness, sit with us.
MACBETH	There's no empty chair.
LENNOX	Here is your reserved seat, sir.
MACBETH	Where?
LENNOX	Here, my lord. What frightens your highness?
MACBETH	Which of you did this?
LORDS	Did what, my lord?
MACBETH	You can't blame me. Don't shake your bloody hair at me.
ROSS	Guests, get up. The king is unwell.
LADY MACBETH	Sit, my friends. My husband is often distressed, a problem he has had from boyhood. Please, sit down. The illusion will pass. After he regains his composure, he will be normal again. If you stare at him, he will be offended. Your notice will lengthen his fit. Eat your dinner and ignore him. Are you returned to normal?

ACT III

TRANSLATION

MACBETH	Ay, and a bold one, that dare look on that Which might appal the devil.
LADY MACBETH	O proper stuff! 60 This is the very painting of your fear; This is the air-drawn dagger which, you said, Led you to Duncan. O! these flaws and starts— Impostors to true fear—would well become A woman's story at a winter's fire, 65 Authoriz'd by her grandam. Shame itself! Why do you make such faces? When all's done, You look but on a stool.
MACBETH	Prithee, see there! behold! look! lo! how say you? Why, what care I? If thou canst nod, speak too. 70 If charnel-houses and our graves must send Those that we bury back, our monuments Shall be the maws of kites. *[Ghost disappears]*
LADY MACBETH	What! quite unmann'd in folly?
MACBETH	If I stand here, I saw him.
LADY MACBETH	Fie, for shame!
MACBETH	Blood hath been shed ere now, i' the olden time, 75 Ere human statute purg'd the gentle weal; Ay, and since too, murders have been perform'd Too terrible for the ear: the times have been, That, when the brains were out, the man would die, And there an end; but now they rise again, 80 With twenty mortal murders on their crowns, And push us from our stools: this is more strange Than such a murder is.
LADY MACBETH	My worthy lord, Your noble friends do lack you.
MACBETH	I do forget, Do not muse at me, my most worthy friends; 85 I have a strange infirmity, which is nothing To those that know me. Come, love and health to all; Then, I'll sit down. Give me some wine; fill full. I drink to the general joy of the whole table. And to our dear friend Banquo, whom we miss; 90 Would he were here! to all, and him, we thirst, And all to all.
LORDS	Our duties, and the pledge. *[Re-enter Ghost]*

ORIGINAL

MACBETH	Yes. Only a bold man could look on a sight that would dismay Satan.
LADY MACBETH	What nonsense! This is a vision derived from fear, like that illusion of a dagger leading you to Duncan's bedroom. Oh, such outbursts and alarms are shams compared to real fear. You are behaving like you heard a scary story told by an old woman at her hearth. Shame on you! Why do you grimace? You are merely gazing at a bench.
MACBETH	Please, look at it! See? Look, what are you saying to me? I don't care what you say. If you can nod, you can also speak. If mortuaries and graves return the dead to earth, our only grave markers will be in the belly of vultures. *[Ghost disappears]*
LADY MACBETH	What is the matter with you? You are belittled by your foolishness.
MACBETH	As I stand here, I saw Banquo.
LADY MACBETH	Shame on you!
MACBETH	Just as murder was committed in the past before laws civilized society, in recent times, the same savagery has happened that is too terrible for words. There was a time that, when brains were beaten from a corpse, the body lay dead. Now, the dead rise again, with twenty gashes on their heads. The sight pushes me off my bench. This appearance is stranger than the assassination itself.
LADY MACBETH	My lord, your guests miss your company.
MACBETH	I had forgotten them. Don't be alarmed, worthy friends. I have a strange mental illness that my close friends are aware of. Come, I pledge affection and health to all. Let's sit down. Pass the wine; fill the cups. I drink to the pleasure of all my guests. And I salute my friend Banquo, whom I miss. I wish he were here. To all of you and to him, let's drink to everybody.
LORDS	We pledge our duty to the king and the health of all. *[Re-enter Ghost]*

ACT III

TRANSLATION

MACBETH	Avaunt! and quit my sight! Let the earth hide thee!
	Thy bones are marrowless, thy blood is cold;
	Thou hast no speculation in those eyes 95
	Which thou dost glare with.

LADY MACBETH   Think of this, good peers,
But as a thing of custom: 'tis no other;
Only it spoils the pleasure of the time.

MACBETH   What man dare, I dare:
Approach thou like the rugged Russian bear, 100
The arm'd rhinoceros, or the Hyrcan tiger;
Take any shape but that, and my firm nerves
Shall never tremble: or be alive again,
And dare me to the desert with thy sword;
If trembling I inhabit then, protest me 105
The baby of a girl. Hence, horrible shadow!
Unreal mockery, hence! *[Ghost vanishes]*
                              Why, so; being gone,
I am a man again. Pray you, sit still.

LADY MACBETH   You have displac'd the mirth, broke the good meeting,
With most admir'd disorder.

MACBETH   Can such things be 110
And overcome us like a summer's cloud,
Without our special wonder? You make me strange
Even to the disposition that I owe,
When now I think you can behold such sights,
And keep the natural ruby of your cheeks, 115
When mine are blanch'd with fear.

ROSS   What sights, my lord?

LADY MACBETH   I pray you, speak not; he grows worse and worse;
Question enrages him. At once, good-night;
Stand not upon the order of your going,
But go at once.

LENNOX   Good-night; and better health 120
Attend his majesty!

LADY MACBETH   A kind good-night to all!
                    [Exeunt Lords and Attendants]

MACBETH   It will have blood, they say; blood will have blood:
Stones have been known to move and trees to speak;
Augures and understand relations have
By maggot-pies and choughs and rooks brought forth 125
The secret'st man of blood. What is the night?

MACBETH   Go away! leave my sight! Let your grave hide you! Your bones have no marrow. Your eyes are cold. You have no intelligence in your eyes, which glare at me.

LADY MACBETH   Good friends, think of this disturbance as ordinary. It is not unusual, but it spoils our pleasant evening.

MACBETH   I accept any challenge that other men face. Approach me like a Russian bear, a thick-skinned rhinoceros, or an Asian tiger. Take any shape you want but that of Banquo and I will not tremble. Come to life again and draw your sword. If I tremble at facing a living man, you may call me a baby girl. Go away, horrible vision! Go away, you mockery of reality! *[Ghost vanishes]* Now that it's gone, I am well again. Please, sit down.

LADY MACBETH   You have ruined the fun and destroyed a good feast with your strange fit.

MACBETH   Can such ghosts hover like a cloud without disturbing me? You make me feel that I do not know myself. How can you see such a ghost and not turn white like me?

ROSS   What ghost, my lord?

LADY MACBETH   Please, don't annoy him. He is becoming more upset. Questioning him only makes him angry. Please, leave. Don't bother with ceremony, but depart at once.

LENNOX   Good night. I hope your majesty will soon feel better.

LADY MACBETH   Good night to you all! *[Lords and servants depart]*

MACBETH   The ghost wants blood. Murder demands more vengeance. Vengeance can move stones and cause trees to talk. Omens of magpies and crows and rooks and their interpretations have summoned the hidden dead. What time is it?

TRANSLATION

LADY MACBETH Almost at odds with morning, which is which.

MACBETH How sayst thou, that Macduff denies his person
At our great bidding?

LADY MACBETH   Did you send to him, sir?

MACBETH I hear it by the way; but I will send.   130
There's not a one of them but in his house
I keep a servant fee'd. I will to-morrow—
And betimes I will—to the weird sisters:
More shall they speak; for now I am bent to know,
By the worst means, the worst. For mine own good   135
All causes shall give way: I am in blood
Stepp'd in so far, that, should I wade no more,
Returning were as tedious as go o'er.
Strange things I have in head that will to hand,
Which must be acted ere they may be scann'd.   140

LADY MACBETH You lack the season of all natures, sleep.

MACBETH Come, we'll to sleep. My strange and self-abuse
Is the initiate fear that wants hard use:
We are yet but young in deed. *[Exeunt]*

ORIGINAL

LADY MACBETH   It is halfway between night and morning.

MACBETH   What is your opinion of Macduff's refusal to answer my call?

LADY MACBETH   Did you send for him?

MACBETH   I have heard that he won't come, but I will summon him anyway. In every noble's house, I keep a spy in my employ. Tomorrow, I will talk with the witches. I must know the worst of my fate, even if I have to consort with evil. For my own advancement, I shall abandon my morals. I have waded so far in blood that wading back is no more difficult than continuing on. I must act on the bizarre thoughts in my mind. I will take action without thinking about the consequences.

LADY MACBETH   Most of all, you need some sleep.

MACBETH   Come, we'll go to bed. My odd self-deception is the kind of fear felt by one accustomed to dealing with terror. *[They depart]*

ACT III

ACT III, SCENE 5

A heath.

[Thunder. Enter the three witches, meeting HECATE]

FIRST WITCH   Why, how now, Hecate! you look angerly.

HECATE   Have I not reason, beldams as you are,
Saucy and overbold? How did you dare
To trade and traffic with Macbeth
In riddles and affairs of death;   5
And I, the mistress of your charms,
The close contriver of all harms,
Was never call'd to bear my part,
Or show the glory of our art?
And, which is worse, all you have done   10
Hath been but for a wayward son,
Spiteful and wrathful; who, as others do,
Loves for his own ends, not for you.
But make amends now: get you gone,
And at the pit of Acheron   15
Meet me i' the morning: thither he
Will come to know his destiny:
Your vessels and your spells provide,
Your charms and every thing beside.
I am for the air; this night I'll spend   20
Unto a dismal and a fatal end:
Great business must be wrought ere noon:
Upon the corner of the moon
There hangs a vaporous drop profound;
I'll catch it ere it come to ground: 25
And that distill'd by magic sleights
Shall raise such artificial sprites
As by the strength of their illusion
Shall draw him on to his confusion:
He shall spurn fate, scorn death, and bear   30
His hopes 'bove wisdom, grace, and fear;
And you all know, security
Is mortals' chiefest enemy.
[Song within, 'Come away, come away,' etc.]
Hark! I am call'd; my little spirit, see,
Sits in a foggy cloud, and stays for me. *[Exit]*   35

FIRST WITCH   Come, let's make haste; she'll soon be back again. *[Exeunt]*

ORIGINAL

ACT III, SCENE 5

A plain.

[Thunder. The three witches enter and encounter HECATE, the moon goddess]

FIRST WITCH   Why are you angry, Hecate!

HECATE   Don't I have reason to be mad at you naughty, daring women. How dare you consort with Macbeth in prophecy and deadly matters without consulting me, the mistress of magic, the secret maker of hexes, the model of the witch's art! Even worse, you have left Macbeth spiteful and angry. He plots evil for his own purpose, not as an offering to you. Make your apologies and be gone. I will meet you in the morning at the pit of hell. He will arrive to know his future. Bring your vessels and magic spells, your charms and anything else you need. I am going to fly away and spend the night working out a calamity. I have business to complete before noon. I must catch a drop hanging from a corner of the moon before it falls. From this magic drop, I will summon spirits that, by the power they cast over Macbeth, shall lure him further toward his doom. He will laugh at fate and death and chase his hopes without giving a thought to wisdom, grace, or fear. As you all know, security is a serious danger to humans. *[Song within, 'Come away, come away']* Listen! I am summoned. My little spirit waits for me on a wisp of fog. *[She departs]*

FIRST WITCH   Let's hurry before she gets back. *[They depart]*

TRANSLATION

ACT III, SCENE 6

Forres. A room in the palace.

[Enter LENNOX and another LORD]

LENNOX
My former speeches have but hit your thoughts,
Which can interpret further: only, I say,
Things have been strangely borne. The gracious Duncan
Was pitied of Macbeth: marry, he was dead:
And the right-valiant Banquo walk'd too late;   5
Whom, you may say, if 't please you, Fleance kill'd
For Fleance fled: men must not walk too late.
Who cannot want the thought how monstrous
It was for Malcolm and for Donalbain
To kill their gracious father? damned fact!   10
How it did grieve Macbeth! did he not straight
In pious rage the two delinquents tear,
That were the slaves of drink and thralls of sleep?
Was not that nobly done? Ay, and wisely too;
For 'twould have anger'd any heart alive   15
To hear the men deny 't. So that, I say,
He has borne all things well; and I do think
That, had he Duncan's sons under his key,—
As an 't please heaven, he shall not,—they should find
What 'twere to kill a father; so should Fleance.   20
But, peace! for from broad words, and 'cause he fail'd
His presence at the tyrant's feast, I hear
Macduff lives in disgrace. Sir, can you tell
Where he bestows himself?

LORD
                   The son of Duncan,
From whom this tyrant holds the due of birth,   25
Lives in the English court, and is receiv'd
Of the most pious Edward with such grace
That the malevolence of fortune nothing
Takes from his high respect. Thither Macduff
Is gone to pray the holy king, upon his aid   30
To wake Northumberland and war-like Siward:
That, by the help of these—with him above
To ratify the work—we may again
Give to our tables meat, sleep to our nights,
Free from our feasts and banquets bloody knives,   35
Do faithful homage and receive free honours;
All which we pine for now. And this report
Hath so exasperate the king that he
Prepares for some attempt of war.

ORIGINAL

ACT III, SCENE 6

Forres. A room in the palace.

[Enter LENNOX and another LORD]

LENNOX What I have said before, you can ponder on. In conclusion, I think affairs in Scotland are strangely managed. Macbeth pitied Duncan, a generous king. But Duncan was dead and couldn't speak for himself. And the brave Banquo was out after dark. You may charge that his son Fleance killed him, then fled. People must not stay out after dark. Doesn't everybody think it monstrous of Malcolm and Donalbain to kill their good father? A damnable act! It grieved Macbeth so much that, in a righteous rage, he murdered the two servants, who were dead drunk. Was Macbeth's act not noble? Yes, and wise. He didn't want anyone to hear the servants deny their part in the assassination. Macbeth appears to have acted well. I think that, if he had Duncan's heirs in jail—and I hope he will never have them there—the sons would suffer for killing their father. Fleance would suffer the same punishment for killing a father. Enough speculation. From rumors, I hear that Macduff disgraced himself at court for not attending the tyrant's feast. Sir, do you know where Macduff is keeping himself?

LORD Malcolm, Duncan's heir, who deserves the throne, lives at the court of Edward, the English king, a pious man known for goodness. Macduff has gone to convince Edward to conspire with the people of Northumberland and with Siward, the earl of Northumberland. If these men join the rebellion that Edward sanctions, Scots may once more eat and sleep well, freed from assassinations and honored for our loyalty. News of Macduff's mission exasperates Macbeth so much that he is getting ready for war.

ACT III

TRANSLATION

LENNOX   Sent he to Macduff?

LORD   He did: and with an absolute, 'Sir, not I,'   40
                 The cloudy messenger turns me his back,
                 And hums, as who should say, 'You'll rue the time
                 That clogs me with this answer.'

LENNOX   And that well might
                 Advise him to a caution to hold what distance
                 His wisdom can provide. Some holy angel   45
                 Fly to the court of England and unfold
                 His message ere he come, that a swift blessing
                 May soon return to this our suffering country
                 Under a hand accurs'd!

LORD   I'll send my prayers with him!
                 [Exeunt]

LENNOX   Did he send for Macduff?

LORD   He did. Macduff replied, "No, sir." The gloomy messenger turns his back and implies that Macbeth will make Macduff sorry for refusing a royal order.

LENNOX   Macduff would be cautious to keep his distance from Macbeth. I wish that an angel might fly to King Edward and explain the real reason that Scotland suffers under a cursed ruler.

LORD   I will pray for Macduff! *[They depart]*

ACT III

ACT IV, SCENE 1

A cavern. In the middle, a boiling cauldron.

[Thunder. Enter the three Witches]

FIRST WITCH	Thrice the brinded cat hath mew'd.
SECOND WITCH	Thrice and once the hedge-pig whin'd,
THIRD WITCH	Harpier cries: 'Tis time, 'tis time.

FIRST WITCH Round about the cauldron go;
In the poison'd entrails throw.   5
Toad, that under cold stone
Days and nights hast thirty-one
Swelter'd venom sleeping got,
Boil thou first i' the charmed pot.

ALL Double, double toil and trouble;   10
Fire burn and cauldron bubble.

SECOND WITCH Fillet of a fenny snake,
In the cauldron boil and bake;
Eye of newt, and toe of frog,
Wool of bat, and tongue of dog,   15
Adder's fork, and blind-worm's sting,
Lizard's leg, and howlet's wing
For a charm of powerful trouble,
Like a hell-broth boil and bubble.

ALL Double, double toil and trouble;   20
Fire burn and cauldron bubble.

THIRD WITCH Scale of dragon, tooth of wolf,
Witches' mummy, maw and gulf
Of the ravin'd salt-sea shark,
Root of hemlock digg'd i' the dark,   25
Liver of blaspheming Jew,
Gall of goat, and slips of yew
Sliver'd in the moon's eclipse,
Nose of Turk, and Tartar's lips,
Finger of birth-strangled babe   30
Ditch-deliver'd by a drab,
Make the gruel thick and slab:
Add there to a tiger's chaudron,
For the ingredients of our cauldron.

ALL Double, double toil and trouble;   35
Fire burn and cauldron bubble.

ORIGINAL

ACT IV, SCENE 1

A cave. In the middle, a boiling pot.

[Thunder. Enter the three Witches]

FIRST WITCH   Three times the mottled cat mewed.

SECOND WITCH   Four times a hedgehog whined.

THIRD WITCH   A demon cries, "It's time, it's time."

FIRST WITCH   Go in a circle around the pot; throw in poisoned guts. Boil first in the magic pot a toad that slept under a cold stone for 31 days to ooze poison.

ALL   Double hardship and trouble; fire burn and make the pot boil.

SECOND WITCH   Slice of a swamp snake cook and boil in the pot. Lizard's eye and frog's toe, bat's wool, and dog's tongue, snake's forked tongue, and the stinger of a worm.

ALL   Double hardship and trouble; fire burn and make the pot boil.

THIRD WITCH   A dragon's scale, wolf's tooth, dried corpse of a witch, stomach and guts of a blood-thirsty sea shark. Hemlock root dug up in the dark. Liver of a sacrilegious Jew, goat's digestive juice, and slivers of an evergreen sliced during an eclipse of the moon. A Turk's nose and a wild Russian's lips, finger of a stillborn baby that a whore gave birth to in a ditch. Make the mix thick and slimy. Add a tiger's guts to the pot to complete the ingredients.

ALL   Double hardship and trouble; fire burn and make the pot boil.

ACT IV

TRANSLATION

SECOND WITCH Cool it with a baboon's blood,
Then the charm is firm and good.
[Enter HECATE]

HECATE O! well done! I commend your pains,
And every one shall share i' the games.
And now about the cauldron sing,
Like elves and fairies in a ring,
Enchanting all that you put in.
[Music and a song, 'Black Spirits,' etc.*]*

SECOND WITCH By the pricking of my thumbs,
Something wicked this way comes.
Open, locks,
Whoever knocks.
[Enter MACBETH]

MACBETH How now, you secret, black, and midnight hags!
What is 't you do?

ALL A deed without a name.

MACBETH I conjure you, by that which you profess,—
Howe'er you come to know it,—answer me:
Though you untie the winds and let them fight
Against the churches; though the yesty waves
Confound and swallow navigation up;
Though bladed corn be lodg'd and trees blown down;
Though castles topple on their warders' heads;
Though palaces and pyramids do slope
Their heads to their foundations; though the treasure
Of Nature's germens tumble all together,
Even till destruction sicken; answer me
To what I ask you.

FIRST WITCH Speak.

SECOND WITCH Demand.

THIRD WITCH We'll answer.

FIRST WITCH Say if thou'dst rather hear it from our mouths,
Or from our masters'?

MACBETH Call 'em: let me see 'em.

FIRST WITCH Pour in sow's blood, that hath eaten
Her nine farrow; grease that's sweaten
From the murderer's gibbet throw
Into the flame.

SECOND WITCH   Cool it with baboon blood to make a firm, dependable magic spell. *[Enter HECATE]*

HECATE   Good work! I compliment your efforts. Each witch shall share in the fun. And now sing around the pot like a circle of elves and fairies to enchant the ingredients. *[Music and a song, 'Black Spirits']*

SECOND WITCH   The prickling on my thumbs warns me that evil is coming. Open, magic atmosphere, and let in the visitor. *[Enter MACBETH]*

MACBETH   Greetings, you dark, plotting, evil hags! What are you doing?

ALL   Our task can't be identified in words.

MACBETH   I summon you, by your magic profession—however you learned it—tell me. Even if you unleash the winds and let them lash churches, even if the foamy waves destroy and sink ships; even if you uproot ripe corn and topple trees; even if you blow down castles on their owners' heads; even if you tilt palaces and pyramids on their founda- tions; even if you destroy seedlings, tell me what I want to know.

ACT IV

FIRST WITCH   Tell us.

SECOND WITCH   Ask what you want.

THIRD WITCH   We will reply.

FIRST WITCH   Tell us whether you prefer prophecies or visions.

MACBETH   Summon them. Let me see your visions.

FIRST WITCH   Add to the flame the blood of a mother pig that has eaten her nine piglets and pour in the sweat from a hanged murderer.

TRANSLATION

ALL	Come, high or low; Thyself and office deftly show. *[Thunder. First Apparition of an armed Head]*
MACBETH	Tell me, thou unknown power,—
FIRST WITCH	He knows thy thought: Hear his speech, but say thou nought. 70
FIRST APPARITION	Macbeth! Macbeth! Macbeth! beware Macduff; Beware the Thane of Fife. Dismiss me. Enough. *[Descends]*
MACBETH	Whate'er thou art, for thy good caution thanks; Thou hast harp'd my fear aright. But one word more,—
FIRST WITCH	He will not be commanded: here's another, 75 More potent than the first. *[Thunder. Second Apparition, a bloody Child]*
SECOND APPARITION	Macbeth! Macbeth! Macbeth!—
MACBETH	Had I three ears, I'd hear thee.
SECOND APPARITION	Be bloody, bold, and resolute; laugh to scorn The power of man, for none of woman born 80 Shall harm Macbeth. *[Descends]*
MACBETH	Then live, Macduff: what need I fear of thee? But yet I'll make assurance double sure, And take a bond of fate: thou shalt not live; That I may tell pale hearted fear it lies, 85 And sleep in spite of thunder. *[Thunder. Third Apparition, a Child crowned, with a tree in his hand]* What is this, That rises like the issue of a king, And wears upon his baby brow the round And top of sovereignty?
ALL	Listen but speak not to 't.
THIRD APPARITION	Be lion-mettled, proud, and take no care 90 Who chafes, who frets, or where conspirers are: Macbeth shall never vanquish'd be until Great Birnam Wood to high Dunsinane Hill Shall come against him. *[Descends]*

ALL	Come from on high or from below earth and show yourself and your purpose. *[Thunder. First vision is a head covered by a helmet]*
MACBETH	Tell me, you unidentified power.
FIRST WITCH	The vision knows what you are thinking. Listen to him, but keep silent.
FIRST APPARITION	Macbeth! Macbeth! Macbeth! Watch out for Macduff, the lord of Fife. Let me go. I have said enough. *[It sinks back into the pot]*
MACBETH	Whatever you are, thanks for the warning. You have spoken my fear of Macduff. But tell me more.
FIRST WITCH	You can't call him back. Here is another vision more powerful than the first vision. *[Thunder. Second vision, a blood-covered child]*
SECOND APPARITION	Macbeth! Macbeth! Macbeth!
MACBETH	I hear you as though I had three ears.
SECOND APPARITION	Be blood-thirsty, daring, and determined. Laugh at human powers, for no one born of woman will harm Macbeth. *[It sinks back into the pot]*
MACBETH	Then I may as well let Macduff live. Why should I fear him? But I want to make doubly certain of my future: I won't let him live. I want to be able to quiet my fear and sleep in spite of omens. *[Thunder. A third vision, a child wearing a crown and carrying a tree in his hand]* What is the meaning of this illusion, which rises from the pot like a baby prince and wears on its head the king's crown?
ALL	Listen to it, but say nothing.
THIRD APPARITION	Be as courageous and proud as a lion and don't worry about the troublesome, complaining conspirators. Macbeth will never fall until the woods at Birnam attack Dunsinane Hill. *[It sinks into the pot]*

ACT IV

MACBETH
　　　　　　　　　　　　　　That will never be:
Who can impress the forest, bid the tree　　　　　　95
Unfix his earth-bound root? Sweet bodements! good!
Rebellion's head, rise never till the wood
Of Birnam rise, and our high-plac'd Macbeth
Shall live the lease of nature, pay his breath
To time and mortal custom. Yet my heart　　　　　100
Throbs to know one thing: tell me—if your art
Can tell so much,—shall Banquo's issue ever
Reign in this kingdom?

ALL
　　　　　　　　　　　Seek to know no more.

MACBETH
I will be satisfied: deny me this,
And an eternal curse fall on you! Let me know.　　　105
Why sinks that cauldron? and what noise is this?
[Hautboys]

FIRST WITCH　Show!

SECOND WITCH　Show!

THIRD WITCH　Show!

ALL
Show his eyes, and grieve his heart;　　　　　　110
Come like shadows, so depart.
*[A show of Eight Kings; the last with a glass
in his hand: BANQUO'S GHOST following]*

MACBETH
Thou art too like the spirit of Banquo; down!
Thy crown does sear mine eyeballs: and thy hair,
Thou other gold-bound brow, is like the first:
A third is like the former. Filthy hags!　　　　　115
Why do you show me this? A fourth! Start, eyes!
What! will the line stretch out to the crack of doom?
Another yet? A seventh! I'll see no more:
And yet the eighth appears, who bears a glass
Which shows me many more; and some I see　　　120
That two-fold balls and treble sceptres carry
Horrible sight! Now, I see, 'tis true;
For the blood-bolter'd Banquo smiles upon me,
And points at them for his. *[Apparitions vanish]*
　　　　　　　　　　　What! is this so?

MACBETH	That will never happen. Who can turn a forest into an army or make a tree pull up its roots? Sweet omens! Good! No one will rebel until Birnam Wood raises a revolt. Macbeth shall retain his throne and live out his life with ease. Still, my heart longs to know, if magic can tell me, whether Banquo's children will ever rule this kingdom?
ALL	Don't try to look farther into the future.
MACBETH	I must satisfy my curiosity. If you refuse, an unending curse will strike you! Tell me. Why is the pot sinking? What is that noise? *[Oboes]*
FIRST WITCH	Appear!
SECOND WITCH	Appear!
THIRD WITCH	Appear!
ALL	Inform his eyes and pain his heart. Come and go like shadows. *[An illusion of Eight Kings. The last carries a mirror in his hand. BANQUO'S GHOST follows the kings]*
MACBETH	You look too much like Banquo's ghost. Go away! Your crown burns my eyes and the hair of the crowned head looks like the first apparition. The third is like the second. Despicable witches, why do you reveal this illusion? A fourth king! My eyes flinch at the sight! And another? A seventh! I don't want to see any more. And an eighth appears carrying a mirror which reflects many more kings. Some carry double globes and three scepters. What a horrible vision! Now I know that the prediction is true because blood-stained Banquo smiles at me and points to the kings as though they are his dynasty. *[The illusion disappears]* Is this a true prediction?

ACT IV

TRANSLATION

FIRST WITCH	Ay, sir, all this is so: but why 125

FIRST WITCH   Ay, sir, all this is so: but why   125
        Stands Macbeth thus amazedly?
        Come sisters, cheer we up his sprites,
        And show the best of our delights.
        I'll charm the air to give a sound,
        While you perform your antick round,   130
        That this great king may kindly say
        Our duties did his welcome pay.
        [Music. The Witches dance, and then
        vanish with HECATE]

MACBETH   Where are they? Gone? Let this pernicious hour
        Stand aye accursed in the calendar!
        Come in, without there!
        [Enter LENNOX]

LENNOX   What's your Grace's will?   135

MACBETH   Saw you the weird sisters?

LENNOX   No, my Lord.

MACBETH   Came they not by you?

LENNOX   No indeed, my Lord.

MACBETH   Infected be the air whereon they ride,
        And damn'd all those that trust them! I did hear
        The galloping of horse: who was 't came by?   140

LENNOX   'Tis two or three, my Lord, that bring you word
        Macduff is fled to England.

MACBETH   Fled to England!

LENNOX   Ay, my good Lord.

MACBETH   Time, thou anticipat'st my dread exploits;
        The flighty purpose never is o'ertook   145
        Unless the deed go with it; from this moment
        The very firstlings of my heart shall be
        The firstlings of my hand. And even now,
        To crown my thoughts with acts, be it thought and done;
        The castle of Macduff I will surprise;   150
        Seize upon Fife; give to the edge of the sword
        His wife, his babes, and all unfortunate souls
        That trace him in his line. No boasting like a fool;
        This deed I'll do before this purpose cool:
        But no more sights! Where are these gentlemen?   155
        Come, bring me where they are. *[Exeunt]*

FIRST WITCH	Yes, the illusions are true. But why does Macbeth seem so shocked? Come, witches, let's cheer his spirit and reveal the best of our powers. I'll create sounds in the air while you dance in a circle so this great king may say that we welcomed him. *[Music. The Witches dance, and then vanish with HECATE]*
MACBETH	Where did they go? Vanished! Let this evil hour be cursed in history! Whoever is outside, come in! *[Enter LENNOX]*
LENNOX	Did you want something?
MACBETH	Did you see the witches?
LENNOX	No, my Lord.
MACBETH	Didn't they pass you at the door?
LENNOX	No indeed, my Lord.
MACBETH	The air through which they fly is contaminated. Anyone who trusts them is doomed. I did hear a horse gallop. Who has arrived?
LENNOX	There are two or three messengers, my lord, who report that Macduff has fled to England.
MACBETH	Fled to England!
LENNOX	Yes, my lord.
MACBETH	There is not time enough to carry out my plots; just planning the act is worthless if I don't have time to do what I must. From now on, whatever comes first in my heart shall be the first act that I complete. Now I must finish the deed I am plotting. I will raid Macduff's castle, capture Fife, and slay his wife and children and anyone who is kin to the Macduffs. Without a word to my credit, I will accomplish this act before I change my mind. Show me no more visions! Where are these visitors? Take me to them. *[They go out]*

ACT IV

TRANSLATION

ACT IV, SCENE 2

Fife. Macduff's castle.

[Enter LADY MACDUFF, her Son, and ROSS]

LADY MACDUFF   What had he done to make him fly the land?

ROSS   You must have patience, madam.

LADY MACDUFF   He had none:
His flight was madness: when our actions do not,
Our fears do make us traitors.

ROSS   You know not
Whether it was his wisdom or his fear.   5

LADY MACDUFF   Wisdom! to leave his wife, to leave his babes,
His mansion and his titles in a place
From whence himself does fly? He loves us not;
He wants the natural touch; for the poor wren,
The most diminutive of birds, will fight—   10
Her young ones in her nest—against the owl.
All is the fear and nothing is the love;
As little is the wisdom, where the flight
So runs against all reason.

ROSS   My dearest coz,
I pray you, school yourself: but, for your husband,   15
He is noble, wise, judicious, and best knows
The fits o' the season. I dare not speak much further:
But cruel are the times, when we are traitors
And do not know ourselves, when we hold rumour
From what we fear, yet know not what we fear,   20
But float upon a wild and violent sea
Each way and move. I take my leave of you:
Shall not be long but I'll be here again.
Things at the worst will cease, or else climb upward
To what they were before. My pretty cousin,   25
Blessing upon you!

LADY MACDUFF   Father'd he is, and yet he's fatherless.

ROSS   I am so much a fool, should I stay longer,
It would be my disgrace, and your discomfort:
I take my leave at once. *[Exit]*

LADY MACDUFF   Sirrah, your father's dead: 30
And what will you do now? How will you live?

ORIGINAL

ACT IV, SCENE 2

Macduff's castle at Fife on Scotland's southeastern coast.

[Enter LADY MACDUFF, her Son, and ROSS]

LADY MACDUFF   What did Macduff do that caused him to run from Scotland?

ROSS   Be patient and you will learn the truth, Madam.

LADY MACDUFF   He did nothing wrong; his departure makes no sense. Even though he was innocent, his fear caused him to betray his country.

ROSS   You can't know whether he left because it was the wise thing to do or because he was afraid.

LADY MACDUFF   Could it be wise to abandon me and his children, his property, and his respected name in Scotland by running away? He lacks the devotion to his family that animals feel. Even a tiny wren, the smallest bird, will fight an owl to protect her babies in the nest. Macduff was more afraid than devoted. There is no wisdom in madly running away from home.

ROSS   My dearest cousin, please control yourself. Macduff is noble and cautious. He understands Scotland's terrors since Macbeth became king. I can't say more. These are cruel times. The dangers reveal aspects of our own character that cringe at rumors of terror even when we don't know whether they are true. Unfounded accusations float this way and that. I am leaving, but I will return soon. The bad days will end or return to the state of the kingdom under Duncan. My pretty cousin, Macduff's son, bless you.

LADY MACDUFF   He has a father, but his father is not here.

ROSS   I am so tender-hearted that, if I stay longer, I will embarrass myself and you by weeping. I must go. *[He goes out]*

LADY MACDUFF   Son, your father's gone. How will you manage? Who will protect you?

ACT IV

TRANSLATION

SON	As birds do, mother.
LADY MACDUFF	What! with worms and flies?
SON	With what I get, I mean; and so do they.
LADY MACDUFF	Poor bird! Thou'dst never fear the net nor lime, The pit-fall nor the gin.
SON	Why should I, mother? Poor birds they are not set for. My father is not dead, for all your saying.
LADY MACDUFF	Yes, he is dead: how wilt thou do for a father?
SON	Nay, how will you do for a husband?
LADY MACDUFF	Why, I can buy me twenty at any market.
SON	Then you'll buy 'em to sell again.
LADY MACDUFF	Thou speak'st with all thy wit; and yet, i' faith, With wit enough for thee.
SON	Was my father a traitor, mother?
LADY MACDUFF	Ay, that he was.
SON	What is a traitor?
LADY MACDUFF	Why, one that swears and lies.
SON	And be all traitors that do so?
LADY MACDUFF	Every one that does so is a traitor, and must be hanged.
SON	And must they all be hanged that swear and lie?
LADY MACDUFF	Every one.
SON	Who must hang them?
LADY MACDUFF	Why, the honest men.
SON	Then the liars and swearers are fools, for there are liars and swearers enow to beat the honest men, and hang up them.
LADY MACDUFF	Now God help thee, poor monkey! But how wilt thou do for a father?
SON	If he were dead, you'd weep for him: if you would not, it were a good sign that I should quickly have a new father.

SON	Like birds, mother.
LADY MACDUFF	By feeding on worms and flies?
SON	Like birds, I will survive on bare essentials.
LADY MACDUFF	My poor little bird, you will never be netted or trapped.
SON	Why should I be caught, Mother? Hunters aren't interested in small birds. And Father is still alive, even though you say he is dead.
LADY MACDUFF	Yes, he is dead. How will you survive?
SON	If he is dead, how will you manage as a widow?
LADY MACDUFF	I can remarry twenty times.
SON	Then you can go into the husband business.
LADY MACDUFF	You are a clever child, but wit won't save you.
SON	Did my father betray the king, Mother?
LADY MACDUFF	Yes, he did.
SON	What crime does a traitor commit?
LADY MACDUFF	A traitor pledges an oath, but doesn't remain true to the pledge.
SON	Is every false swearer a traitor?
LADY MACDUFF	Anyone who swears and lies must be executed.
SON	And do all swearers and liars go to the gallows?
LADY MACDUFF	Yes, every one.
SON	Who executes them?
LADY MACDUFF	The hangmen are honest men.
SON	Then traitors are foolish. If they formed an army, they could beat and execute the hangmen.
LADY MACDUFF	God help you, my little monkey. How will you manage without your father?
SON	If he were really dead, you would be weeping now. If you don't cry, then I know that you will soon remarry.

ACT IV

TRANSLATION

LADY MACDUFF   Poor prattler, how thou talk'st!   60
      [Enter a Messenger]

MESSENGER   Bless you, fair dame! I am not to you known,
    Though in your state of honour I am perfect.
    I doubt some danger does approach you nearly:
    If you will take a homely man's advice,
    Be not found here; hence, with your little ones.   65
    To fright you thus, methinks, I am too savage;
    To do worse to you were fell cruelty,
    Which is too nigh your person. Heaven preserve you!
    I dare abide no longer. *[Exit]*

LADY MACDUFF   Whither should I fly?
    I have done no harm. But I remember now   70
    I am in this earthly world, where to do harm
    Is often laudable, to do good sometime
    Accounted dangerous folly; why then, alas!
    Do I put up that womanly defence,
    To say I have done no harm?
    [Enter Murderers]
                   What are these faces?   75

MURDERER   Where is your husband?

LADY MACDUFF   I hope in no place so unsanctified
    Where such as thou mayst find him.

MURDERER   He's a traitor.

SON   Thou liest, thou shag-ear'd villain.

MURDERER   What, you egg!
    Young fry of treachery! *[Stabbing him]*

SON   He has killed me, mother: 80
    Run away, I pray you! *[Dies]*
    [Exit LADY MACDUFF, crying 'Murder!'
    and pursued by the Murderers]

LADY MACDUFF Poor babbler, how you do talk! *[Enter a Messenger]*

MESSENGER My blessings, Lady Macduff! You don't know me, but I am aware of your rank. I suspect danger is coming. If you will take an ordinary man's word, leave here at once with your children. I am cruel to scare you, but worse savagery is coming. Danger is too close. Heaven help you! I can't stay any longer. *[He goes out]*

LADY MACDUFF Where should I escape to? I have done nothing wrong. But in the real world, evil people often are praised and good people often seem foolish. It is too bad! Can I act like a woman by pleading that I am innocent? *[Enter Murderers]* Who are these unknown men?

MURDERER Where is your husband?

LADY MACDUFF I hope he is in a safe place where you can't find him.

MURDERER He's a traitor.

SON You're a liar, you dog-eared criminal.

MURDERER You smart-mouthed kid! The son of a traitor! *[Stabbing him]*

SON I am dying, mother. Run, please, while you can*! [Dies] [Exit LADY MACDUFF, crying 'Murder!' and pursued by the Murderers]*

ACT IV

ACT IV, SCENE 3

England. Before the king's palace.

[Enter MALCOLM and MACDUFF]

MALCOLM	Let us seek out some desolate shade, and there
Weep our sad bosoms empty.

MACDUFF   Let us rather
Hold fast the mortal sword, and like good men
Bestride our down-fall'n birthdom; each new morn
New widows howl, new orphans cry, new sorrows   5
Strike heaven on the face, that it resounds
As if it felt with Scotland and yell'd out
Like syllable of dolour.

MALCOLM   What I believe I'll wail,
What know believe; and what I can redress,
As I shall find the time to friend, I will.   10
What you have spoke, it may be so perchance.
This tyrant, whose sole name blisters our tongues,
Was once thought honest; you have lov'd him well;
He hath not touch'd you yet. I am young; but something
You may deserve of him through me, and wisdom   15
To offer up a weak, poor, innocent lamb
To appease an angry god.

MACDUFF I am not treacherous.

MALCOLM   But Macbeth is.
A good and virtuous nature may recoil
In an imperial charge. But I shall crave your pardon;   20
That which you are my thoughts cannot transpose;
Angels are bright still, though the brightest fell;
Though all things foul would wear the brows of grace,
Yet grace must still look so.

MACDUFF   I have lost my hopes.

MALCOLM Perchance even there where I did find my doubts.   25
Why in that rawness left you wife and child—
Those precious motives, those strong knots of love—
Without leave-taking? I pray you,
Let not my jealousies be your dishonours,
But mine own safeties: you may be rightly just,   30
Whatever I shall think.

ORIGINAL

ACT IV, SCENE 3

In England in front of King Edward's palace.

[Enter MALCOLM and MACDUFF]

MALCOLM   Let us find some shadowed spot and privately share our sorrow over Scotland's hard times.

MACDUFF   No, we should grasp our swords and, like good Scots, march back to Scotland to rid it of an unworthy king. Every day, more women are widowed and their children orphaned. Each day, more grief echoes through Scotland.

MALCOLM   I will mourn for this terrible state of affairs. I will rid Scotland of evil when I am ready. What you have reported may be true. Macbeth may be a tyrant, even though he once had a reputation for honor. You have been loyal to him. He hasn't harmed you, so you have no reason to make up stories about him. I am inexperienced, but you may be testing me for Macbeth's sake. You may betray me to the king like a lamb before an angry god.

MACDUFF   I am not a deceiver.

MALCOLM   But Macbeth is. Even a man of good character may change when he becomes king. I apologize. I can't know for sure whether you are trustworthy. Even the angel Lucifer was once bright before he fell from heaven. Some conniving men are still able to disguise their aims beneath an honorable appearance.

MACDUFF   I have given up hope of convincing you.

MALCOLM   Maybe your despair will convince me. Why did you leave your wife and children in such a dangerous country? How could you leave your loved ones without telling them of your departure? Please, don't let my suspicion demean you. I must be sure of my actions. You may be right. I will have to think about your words.

ACT IV

MACDUFF   Bleed, bleed, poor country!
                   Great tyranny, lay thou thy basis sure,
                   For goodness dare not check thee! wear thou thy wrongs;
                   The title is affeer'd! Fare thee well, lord:
                   I would not be the villain that thou think'st   35
                   For the whole space that's in the tyrant's grasp,
                   And the rich East to boot.

MALCOLM   Be not offended:
                   I speak not as in absolute fear of you.
                   I think our country sinks beneath the yoke;
                   It weeps, it bleeds, and each new day a gash   40
                   Is added to her wounds: I think withal
                   There would be hands uplifted in my right;
                   And here from gracious England have I offer
                   Of goodly thousands: but, for all this,
                   When I shall tread upon the tyrant's head,   45
                   Or wear it on my sword, yet my poor country
                   Shall have more vices than it had before,
                   More suffer, and more sundry ways than ever,
                   By him that shall succeed.

MACDUFF   What should he be?

MALCOLM   It is myself I mean; in whom I know   50
                   All the particulars of vice so grafted,
                   That, when they shall be open'd, black Macbeth
                   Will seem as pure as snow, and the poor state
                   Esteem him as a lamb, being compar'd
                   With my confineless harms.

MACDUFF   Not in the legions   55
                   Of horrid hell can come a devil more damn'd
                   In evils to top Macbeth.

MALCOLM   I grant him bloody,
                   Luxurious, avaricious, false, deceitful,
                   Sudden, malicious, smacking of every sin
                   That has a name; but there's no bottom, none,   60
                   In my voluptuousness: your wives, your daughters,
                   Your matrons, and your maids, could not fill up
                   The cistern of my lust, and my desire
                   All continent impediments would o'erbear
                   That did oppose my will; better Macbeth   65
                   That such an one to reign.

MACDUFF   Poor Scotland is bleeding! Tyrants like Macbeth thrive when good people do nothing to stop them! Because he is king, he can flaunt his evil deeds! Goodbye, Malcolm. I would never be the criminal you think I am, even if crime offered me all of Scotland and Asia.

MALCOLM   Don't take offense. I have no fear of you. I know that Scotland is enslaved. It suffers and sorrows. Each day, a new crime grieves the country more. I believe that others will support my revolt against Macbeth. King Edward has promised me thousands of warriors. But even with an army, when I stamp on Macbeth's crown or lift his severed head on my sword, even then, evil will thrive in Scotland. The people will suffer in more ways under the next king who comes to the throne.

MACDUFF   Could there be a worse king than Macbeth?

MALCOLM   I am referring to myself. I have so many evil habits that, by comparison, Macbeth will seem as white as snow. And Scotland will remember him as a lamb when they compare his reign to mine.

MACDUFF   Not even the souls doomed to hell can be more damned than Macbeth.

MALCOLM   I agree. He is violent, lustful, greedy, dishonest, sneaky, unpredictable, evil, guilty of every sin you can name. However, there is no satisfying my lust. Your wives and daughters, old women and young, can't satisfy my longing for women. No obstacle can halt my willfulness. You are better off under Macbeth than under my rule.

ACT IV

MACDUFF   Boundless intemperance
In nature is a tyranny; it hath been
Th' untimely emptying of the happy throne,
And fall of many kings. But fear not yet
To take upon you what is yours; you may   70
Convey your pleasures in a spacious plenty,
And yet seem cold, the time you may so hoodwink.
We have willing dames enough; there cannot be
That vulture in you, to devour so many
As will to greatness dedicate themselves,   75
Finding it so inclin'd.

MALCOLM   With this there grows
In my most ill-compos'd affection such
A stanchless avarice that, were I king,
I should cut off the nobles for their lands,
Desire his jewels and his other's house;   80
And my more-having would be as a sauce
To make me hunger more, that I should forge
Quarrels unjust against the good and loyal,
Destroying them for wealth.

MACDUFF   This avarice
Sticks deeper, grows with more pernicious root   85
Than summer-seeming lust, and it hath been
The sword of our slain kings: yet do not fear;
Scotland hath foisons to fill up your will,
Of your mere own; all these are portable,
With other graces weigh'd.   90

MALCOLM   But I have none: the king-becoming graces,
As justice, verity, temperance, stableness,
Bounty, perseverance, mercy, lowliness,
Devotion, patience, courage, fortitude,
I have no relish of them, but abound   95
In the division of each several crime,
Acting it many ways. Nay, had I power, I should
Pour the sweet milk of concord into hell,
Uproar the universal peace, confound
All unity on earth.

MACDUFF   O Scotland, Scotland!   100

MALCOLM   If such a one be fit to govern, speak:
I am as I have spoken.

MACDUFF	You are right. Uncontrolled greed has cost us Duncan, a good king, as well as many other monarchs in the past. But don't hesitate to seize the throne that rightfully belongs to you. As king, you can achieve your will. There will be plenty of women to fulfill your lust in private. You can't be so fearful a vulture as to gobble up all those who are willing to sacrifice themselves to you.
MALCOLM	I am so sin-ridden that, if I were king, I would steal land from the nobles and take their jewels and residences. Getting more would make me want more. I would encourage fights between good and loyal citizens and then seize their property.
MACDUFF	Such greed is deep-rooted and fast-growing. It is greed that killed past kings of Scotland. But, don't worry. Scotland has enough royal treasure to content you. We can tolerate your sins because you have so many more good qualities.
MALCOLM	But I have no good qualities. The royal character consists of justice, truth, self-control, stability, generosity, determination, mercy, humility, dedication, patience, bravery, courage. I have none of these. I am blessed with all sorts of criminal urges. If I could, I would dump peace into hell, destroy world contentment, and ruin all harmony on earth.
MACDUFF	Oh, poor Scotland, Scotland!
MALCOLM	If such a person is suited to the throne, say so! My character is exactly as I have described.

ACT IV

MACDUFF
                                    Fit to govern!
No, not to live. O nation miserable,
With an untitled tyrant bloody-scepter'd,
When shalt thou see thy wholesome days again,   105
Since that the truest issue of thy throne
By his own interdiction stands accurs'd,
And does blaspheme his breed? Thy royal father
Was a most sainted king; the queen that bore thee,
Oft'ner upon her knees than on her feet,   110
Died every day she liv'd. Fare thee well!
These evils thou repeat'st upon thyself
Have banish'd me from Scotland. O my breast,
Thy hope ends here!

MALCOLM
                                    Macduff, this noble passion,
Child of integrity, hath from my soul   115
Wip'd the black scruples, reconcil'd my thoughts
To thy good truth and honour. Devilish Macbeth
By many of these trains hath sought to win me
Into his power, and modest wisdom plucks me
From over-credulous haste; but God above   120
Deal between thee and me! for even now
I put myself to thy direction, and
Unspeak mine own detraction, here abjure
The taints and blames I laid upon myself,
For strangers to my nature. I am yet   125
Unknown to woman, never was forsworn,
Scarcely have coveted what was mine own;
At no time broke my faith, would not betray
The devil to his fellow, and delight
No less in truth than life; my first false speaking   130
Was this upon myself. What I am truly,
Is thine and my poor country's to command;
Whither indeed, before thy here-approach,
Old Siward, with ten thousand war-like men,
Already at a point, was setting forth.   135
Now we'll together, and the chance of goodness
Be like our warranted quarrel. Why are you silent?

MACDUFF
Such welcome and unwelcome things at once
'Tis hard to reconcile.
[Enter a Doctor]

MALCOLM
Well; more anon. Comes the king forth, I pray you?   140

MACDUFF	Fit to rule? You aren't fit to live. O wretched Scotland, with a murderous usurper on the throne, when will you see prosperous times again. Even the crown prince by his own admission is not a fit successor to Macbeth. He shames his dynasty. Your father Duncan was a saint; the queen, your mother, spent more time kneeling in prayer and confession than in standing. Farewell. The sins that you claim have ended my residence in Scotland. Oh my heart, there is no hope of better times.
MALCOLM	Macduff, your deep grief, born of honesty, has cleansed me of doubt and proved to me that you are truthful and honorable. Devious Macbeth by trickery has tried to lure me into his grasp. Caution keeps me from giving in to him too quickly. As God will judge, I choose to accept your report. I admit that those sins and faults were made-up. I am still a virgin, have never lied, rarely envied other people's wealth, never betrayed anyone and would not betray, and I value truth over life itself. I was making up those sins for a purpose. I am eager to serve you and Scotland. Before you arrived, Siward the Elder was departing from England at the head of ten thousand soldiers. You and I will fight Macbeth together. May we be lucky enough to prove ourselves worthy. Why don't you answer?
MACDUFF	Your terrible self-description and your news of a revolt against Scotland are bewildering to me. *[Enter a Doctor]*
MALCOLM	We will talk more later. Is King Edward approaching?

ACT IV

TRANSLATION

DOCTOR	Ay, sir; there are a crew of wretched souls That stay his cure; their malady convinces The great assay of art; but, at his touch, Such sanctity hath heaven given his hand, They presently amend.

MALCOLM   I thank you, doctor.   145
[Exit Doctor]

MACDUFF   What's the disease he means?

MALCOLM   'Tis called the evil:
A most miraculous work in this good king,
Which often, since my here-remain in England,
I have seen him do. How he solicits heaven,
Himself best knows; but strangely-visited people,   150
All swoln and ulcerous, pitiful to the eye,
The mere despair of surgery, he cures,
Hanging a golden stamp about their necks,
Put on with holy prayers; and 'tis spoken,
To the succeeding royalty he leaves   155
The healing benediction. With this strange virtue,
He hath a heavenly gift of prophecy,
And sundry blessings hang about his throne
That speak him full of grace.
[Enter ROSS]

MACDUFF   See, who comes here?

MALCOLM   My countryman; but yet I know him not.   160

MACDUFF   My ever-gentle cousin, welcome hither.

MALCOLM   I know him now. Good God, betimes remove
The means that makes us strangers!

ROSS   Sir, amen.

MACDUFF   Stands Scotland where it did?

ROSS   Alas! poor country;
Almost afraid to know itself. It cannot   165
Be call'd our mother, but our grave; where nothing,
But who knows nothing, is once seen to smile;
Where sighs and groans and shrieks that rent the air
Are made, not mark'd; where violent sorrow seems
A modern ecstacy; the dead man's knell   170
Is there scarce ask'd for who; and good men's lives
Expire before the flowers in their caps
Dying or ere they sicken.

DOCTOR	Yes. There is a horde of sick people that wait for him to cure them. Their disease responds to his power. When he touches them, there is such righteousness in his hand that they soon recover their health.
MALCOLM	Thank you for the explanation, doctor. *[The doctor goes out]*
MACDUFF	What disease is he referring to?
MALCOLM	It is called an "evil." It is a miracle that King Edward often performs. I have witnessed the cures during my stay in England. He prays to God and cures these pathetic patients, who suffer tubercular swellings and sores that surgery can't heal. He hangs a gold charm about their necks and prays for them. His powerful blessing will pass to the next kings of England. With this unusual power comes the gift of prophecy. His reign has earned many blessings and much admiration. *[Enter ROSS]*
MACDUFF	Who is coming?
MALCOLM	A Scot, but I don't recognize him.
MACDUFF	It's my cousin. Come in.
MALCOLM	Now I recognize him. Being away from home has made my fellow countrymen strangers to me.
ROSS	Sir, it is true.
MACDUFF	Has Scotland changed since I left?
ROSS	It was once our motherland; now it's our grave. People pretend to know nothing. There is no reason to smile. People make no comment about suffering and cries of terror. Grief for troubles is a common passion. Citizens don't even ask who has died. Good people die without even getting sick.

ACT IV

TRANSLATION

MACDUFF
O! relation
Too nice, and yet too true!

MALCOLM
What's the newest brief?

ROSS
That of an hour's age doth hiss the speaker;   175
Each minute teems a new one.

MACDUFF
How does my wife?

ROSS
Why, well.

MACDUFF
And all my children?

ROSS
Well too.

MACDUFF
The tyrant has not batter'd at their peace?

ROSS
No; they were well at peace when I did leave 'em.

MACDUFF
Be not a niggard of your speech: how goes 't?   180

ROSS
When I came hither to transport the tidings,
Which I have heavily borne, there ran a rumour
Of many worthy fellows that were out;
Which was to my belief witness'd the rather
For that I saw the tyrant's power a-foot.   185
Now is the time of help; your eye in Scotland
Would create soldiers, make our women fight,
To doff their dire distresses.

MALCOLM
Be 't their comfort
We are coming thither. Gracious England hath
Lent us good Siward and ten thousand men;   190
An older and a better soldier none
That Christendom gives out.

ROSS
Would I could answer
This comfort with the like! But I have words
That would be howl'd out in the desert air,
Where hearing should not latch them.

MACDUFF
What concern they?   195
The general cause? or is it a fee-grief
Due to some single breast?

ROSS
No mind that's honest
But in it shares some woe, though the main part
Pertains to you alone.

MACDUFF
If it be mine
Keep it not from me; quickly let me have it.   200

ORIGINAL

MACDUFF   Your words are too detailed, but the truth is necessary.

MALCOLM   What's the latest news?

ROSS   Before an hour passes, new terrors occur.

MACDUFF   How is my wife?

ROSS   Why, she is well.

MACDUFF   And my children?

ROSS   They, too, are well.

MACDUFF   Macbeth has not threatened them?

ROSS   No. They were safe when I left your home.

MACDUFF   Don't be stingy with your words. What is the truth?

ROSS   When I left for England to bring news of Scotland, there was a rumor that worthy rebels were marching. I believed the rumor because I saw Macbeth's soldiers marching. It is time for a revolt. If Scots saw you, more would join the rebels. Even women would fight to rid themselves of their troubles.

MALCOLM   We are coming home to comfort them. Kind Edward has loaned us Siward the Elder and ten thousand troops. Siward is the best and most experienced soldier in the Christian world.

ROSS   I wish that your words consoled me. Unfortunately, I have news that should be howled in the desert where no ear could hear.

MACDUFF   What is the subject? All of Scotland? Or is it a personal grief?

ROSS   Everyone will grieve at this news, even though it refers specifically to Macduff.

MACDUFF   If the report is for me, tell me quickly.

ACT IV

TRANSLATION

ROSS	Let not your ears despise my tongue for ever,
	Which shall possess them with the heaviest sound
	That ever yet they heard.

| MACDUFF | Hum! I guess at it. |

ROSS	Your castle is surpris'd; your wife and babes
	Savagely slaughter'd; to relate the manner,	205
	Were, on the quarry of these murder'd deer,
	To add the death of you.

MALCOLM	Merciful heaven!
	What! man; ne'er pull your hat upon your brows;
	Give sorrow words; the grief that does not speak
	Whispers the o'er-fraught heart and bids it break.	210

| MACDUFF | My children too? |

| ROSS | Wife, children, servants, all |
| | That could be found. |

| MACDUFF | And I must be from thence! |
| | My wife kill'd too? |

| ROSS | I have said. |

MALCOLM	Be comforted:
	Let's make us medicine of our great revenge,
	To cure this deadly grief.	215

MACDUFF	He has no children. All my pretty ones?
	Did you say all? O hell-kite! All?
	What! All my pretty chickens and their dam
	At one fell swoop?

| MALCOLM | Dispute it like a man. |

MACDUFF	I shall do so;	220
	But I must also feel it as a man:
	I cannot but remember such things were,
	That were most precious to me. Did heaven look on,
	And would not take their part? Sinful Macduff!
	They were all struck for thee. Naught that I am,	225
	Not for their own demerits, but for mine,
	Fell slaughter on their souls. Heaven rest them now!

| MALCOLM | Be this the whetstone of your sword: let grief |
| | Convert to anger; blunt not the heart, enrage it. |

ROSS	Don't hate me for telling you the worst news you have ever heard.
MACDUFF	I think I know.
ROSS	Assassins raided your castle, murdered your wife and children savagely like deer. To reveal the details would kill you.
MALCOLM	Merciful heaven! Please, Ross, don't pull your hat down over your face. Tell us the rest. The terror that you don't describe causes Macduff to imagine more heartbreaking scenes.
MACDUFF	My children are also dead?
ROSS	The assassins killed your wife, your children, and all the servants they could find.
MACDUFF	And I was away when it happened! My wife is dead too?
ROSS	Just as I described it.
MALCOLM	Take comfort. Let us turn our urge for vengeance into the cure for Scotland's grief.
MACDUFF	Macbeth has no children. All my little ones? Did you say all of them? Oh hell-hawk! Every one of them? Can it be that my wife and children died in one attack?
MALCOLM	Bear your grief like a man.
MACDUFF	I will bear it like a man, but I must also suffer it like a man. I can't think about the slaughter of my precious family. Did God look down and do nothing to protect them? It is my fault! They died because I left Scotland. They didn't deserve to die. Macbeth slew them in anger at me. God give them rest!
MALCOLM	Let grief sharpen your sword. Let sorrow turn into anger and enrage the heart.

ACT IV

TRANSLATION

| MACDUFF | O! I could play the woman with mine eyes, | 230 |

MACDUFF   O! I could play the woman with mine eyes,   230
                    And braggart with my tongue. But, gentle heavens,
                    Cut short all intermission; front to front
                    Bring thou this fiend of Scotland and myself;
                    Within my sword's length set him; if he 'scape,
                    Heaven forgive him too!

MALCOLM   This tune goes manly.   235
                    Come, go we to the king; our power is ready;
                    Our lack is nothing but our leave. Macbeth
                    Is ripe for shaking, and the powers above
                    Put on their instruments. Receive what cheer you may;
                    The night is long that never finds the day. *[Exeunt]*   240

MACDUFF   Oh, I could weep like a woman and rave over my loss. Oh, God, bring me quickly to confront Macbeth. Bring me face to face with Scotland's fiend. Let us stand sword to sword. If he escapes, God forgive him.

MALCOLM   Your words sound manly. Come, let's speak to King Edward. Our forces are ready. We lack nothing but our departure from England. Macbeth is ready to be unseated. God is arming for war. Take what comfort you can. No night is so long that it never turns into day.
[They go out]

ACT IV

ACT V, SCENE 1

Dunsinane. A room in the castle.

[Enter a Doctor of Physic and a Waiting-Gentlewoman]

DOCTOR   I have two nights watched with you, but can perceive
no truth in your report. When was it she last walked?

GENTLEWOMAN   Since his majesty went into the field, I have seen her
rise from her bed, throw her night gown upon her,
unlock her closet, take forth paper, fold it, write upon   5
't, read it, afterwards seal it, and again return to bed;
yet all this while in a most fast sleep.

DOCTOR   A great perturbation in nature, to receive at once the benefit
of sleep and do the effects of watching! In this slumbery
agitation, besides her walking and other actual   10
performances, what, at any time, have you heard her say?

GENTLEWOMAN   That, sir, which I will not report after her.

DOCTOR   You may to me, and 'tis most meet you should.

GENTLEWOMAN   Neither to you nor any one, having no witness
    to confirm my speech.   15
[Enter LADY MACBETH, with a taper]
Lo you! here she comes. This is her very guise; and,
upon my life, fast asleep. Observe her; stand close.

DOCTOR   How came she by that light?

GENTLEWOMAN   Why, it stood by her: she has light by
her continually; 'tis her command.   20

DOCTOR   You see, her eyes are open.

GENTLEWOMAN   Ay, but their sense is shut.

DOCTOR   What is it she does now? Look, how she rubs her hands.

GENTLEWOMAN   It is an accustomed action with her, to seem thus washing
her hands. I have known her to continue in this a quarter   25
of an hour.

LADY MACBETH   Yet here's a spot.

DOCTOR   Hark! she speaks. I will set down what comes from her,
to satisfy my remembrance the more strongly.

ACT V, SCENE 1

A room in Macbeth's castle at Dunsinane on the
northeastern coast of Scotland.

[Entering are a physician and a lady-in-waiting]

DOCTOR   You and I have watched Lady Macbeth for two nights, but I can't confirm your report. When did she last sleepwalk?

GENTLEWOMAN   When Macbeth last went into combat with his soldiers, I saw her get out of bed, put a robe around her, unlock the closet, take paper, fold it, write on it, read it, seal it, then return to bed. She did all this while fast asleep.

DOCTOR   This suggests a disturbed mind to sleep while seeming to be awake! In her nighttime agitation, besides walking and other odd behaviors, what did she say?

GENTLEWOMAN   I won't reveal what she said.

DOCTOR   It is proper that you tell me.

GENTLEWOMAN   I won't tell you or anybody else without a witness to confirm my report. *[LADY MACBETH enters with a slender candle]* Look, here she comes! This is her nightly pattern. I vow on my life that she is fast asleep. Look at her; come close.

DOCTOR   Where did she get the candle?

GENTLEWOMAN   It was beside her bed. She demands that there be a light burning beside her always.

DOCTOR   Look. Her eyes are open.

GENTLEWOMAN   Yes, but her mind is asleep.

DOCTOR   What is she doing now? Look, she is rubbing her hands.

GENTLEWOMAN   It is her custom to pretend to wash her hands. I have seen her doing it for fifteen minutes at a time.

LADY MACBETH   There's still a spot.

DOCTOR   Listen, she is speaking. I will write down what she says to bolster my memory.

TRANSLATION

LADY MACBETH Out, damned spot! out, I say! One; two: why, then 'tis time   30
to do 't. Hell is murky! Fie, my Lord, fie! a soldier, and
afeard? What need we fear who knows it, when none can
call our power to account? Yet who would have thought
the old man to have had so much blood in him?   35

DOCTOR Do you mark that?

LADY MACBETH The Thane of Fife had a wife: where is she now?
What! will these hands ne'er be clean? No more o' that,
my Lord, no more o' that: you mar all with this starting.

DOCTOR Go to, go to; you have known what you should not.   40

GENTLEWOMAN She has spoke what she should not, I am sure
of that: Heaven knows what she has known.

LADY MACBETH Here's the smell of the blood still: all the perfumes of
Arabia will not sweeten this little hand. Oh! oh! oh!

DOCTOR What a sigh is there! The heart is sorely charged.   45

GENTLEWOMAN I would not have such a heart in my
bosom for the dignity of the whole body.

DOCTOR Well, well, well.

GENTLEWOMAN Pray God it be, sir.

DOCTOR This disease is beyond my practice: yet I have known   50
those which have walked in their sleep who have died
holily in their beds.

LADY MACBETH Wash your hands, put on your night-gown; look not so pale.
I tell you yet again, Banquo's buried; he cannot come out
on 's grave.   55

DOCTOR Even so?

LADY MACBETH To bed, to bed: there's knocking at the gate.
Come, come, come, come, give me your hand.
What's done cannot be undone. To bed, to bed, to bed.
[Exit]

DOCTOR Will she go now to bed?   60

ORIGINAL

LADY MACBETH Out, cursed stain, out I tell you! One o'clock, two o'clock. It is time to do it. Hell is foggy! Shame, my lord, shame! A soldier and scared? Why should we fear getting caught, where no one can challenge the next king? Who could have guessed that the old king would bleed so heavily?

DOCTOR Did you hear that?

LADY MACBETH Macduff, the thane of Fife, had a wife. Where is she now? Will I never wash my hands clean? No more staring, my lord, no more. You will ruin our plans with your flinching.

DOCTOR Shame, shame. You have information that you should not know.

GENTLEWOMAN She has revealed what she should not tell, I am sure. Heaven knows what is in her mind.

LADY MACBETH My hand still smells like blood. All the perfume in Arabia can't freshen it. Oh, oh, oh!

DOCTOR What a weighty sigh! Her heart is terribly burdened.

GENTLEWOMAN I wouldn't have so guilty a heart in my chest. It would dishonor my whole body.

DOCTOR Well, well, well.

GENTLEWOMAN I hope to God that all is well, sir.

DOCTOR I can't cure her ailment. Still, I have known sleepwalkers who have died blamelessly in their beds.

LADY MACBETH Wash your hands, put on your nightshirt; don't look so pale. I have told you that Banquo is dead and buried. He can't escape his grave.

DOCTOR This too?

LADY MACBETH Get to bed. There's knocking at the gate. Come, come, give me your hand. What we have done we can't change. Let's get to bed. *[She goes out]*

DOCTOR Will she go back to bed now?

ACT V

GENTLEWOMAN Directly.

DOCTOR Foul whisperings are abroad. Unnatural deeds
Do breed unnatural troubles; infected minds
To their deaf pillows will discharge their secrets;
More needs she the divine than the physician. 65
God, God forgive us all! Look after her;
Remove from her the means of all annoyance,
And still keep eyes upon her. So, good-night:
My mind she has mated, and amaz'd sight.
I think, but dare not speak. 70

GENTLEWOMAN Good-night, good Doctor. *[Exeunt]*

GENTLEWOMAN Immediately.

DOCTOR Evil rumors are circulating. Crimes cause unusual mental distress. Troubled spirits whisper their secrets in the night. She needs God more than she needs a doctor. May God forgive us all. Take care of her. Keep her from committing suicide. Good night to you. She has baffled my mind and amazed my eyes. I think I understand her troubles, but it is too dangerous to tell anyone.

GENTLEWOMAN Good night, sir. *[They depart]*

ACT V, SCENE 2

The country near Dunsinane.

[Enter, with drum and colours, MENTEITH, CAITHNESS, ANGUS, LENNOX, and Soldiers]

MENTEITH   The English power is near, led on by Malcolm,
His uncle Siward, and the good Macduff.
Revenges burn in them; for their dear causes
Would to the bleeding and the grim alarm
Excite the mortified man.

ANGUS   Near Birnam wood   5
Shall we well meet them; that way are they coming.

CAITHNESS   Who knows if Donalbain be with his brother?

LENNOX   For certain, sir, he is not: I have a file
Of all the gentry: there is Siward's son,
And many unrough youths that even now   10
Protest their first of manhood.

MENTEITH   What does the tyrant?

CAITHNESS   Great Dunsinane he strongly fortifies.
Some say he's mad; others that lesser hate him
Do call it valiant fury; but, for certain,
He cannot buckle his distemper'd cause   15
Within the belt of rule.

ANGUS   .   Now does he feel
His secret murders sticking on his hands;
Now minutely revolts upbraid his faith-breach;
Those he commands move only in command,
Nothing in love; now does he feel his title   20
Hang loose about him, like a giant's robe
Upon a dwarfish thief.

MENTEITH   Who then shall blame
His pester'd senses to recoil and start,
When all that is within him does condemn
Itself for being there?

ACT V, SCENE 2

The territory around Dunsinane.

[MENTEITH, CAITHNESS, ANGUS, LENNOX, and troops enter with a drummer and flag bearers]

MENTEITH   The English army is approaching led by Malcolm, Siward the Elder, and Macduff. They seethe with hatred. Their charges against Macbeth could arouse the dead to arms.

ANGUS   We should meet the army near Birnam wood. That is the direction they are marching.

CAITHNESS   Does anyone know if Donalbain is accompanying his brother Malcolm?

LENNOX   He is for certain not among them. I have a list of nobles, which includes Siward the Younger and many inexperienced lads who are just entering manhood.

MENTEITH   What is the tyrant Macbeth doing?

CAITHNESS   Some say he is crazy; others who hate him less say he displays a courageous fury. It is certain that he can't restore his disorderly rule.

ANGUS   He suffers from revelations of his secret murders. Every minute, rebels charge him with killing King Duncan. His soldiers obey his command, but not out of love for the king. His royal title no longer fits so evil a small-minded criminal.

MENTEITH   Who could blame him for flinching and cowering when his conscience blames him for stealing the throne?

ACT V

TRANSLATION

CAITHNESS   Well, march we on,   25
To give obedience where 'tis truly ow'd;
Meet we the medicine of the sickly weal,
And with him pour we in our country's purge
Each drop of us.

LENNOX   Or so much as it needs
To dew the sovereign flower and drown the weeds.   30
Make we our march towards Birnam.
[Exeunt, marching]

CAITHNESS   Let's march on in obedience to the true crown prince and become the medicine that will cure Scotland.

LENNOX   Whatever the country needs to freshen Duncan's successor and drown the weed who seized the throne. Let's press on to Birnam wood. *[They march out]*

ACT V, SCENE 3

Dunsinane. A room in the castle.

[Enter MACBETH, Doctor, and Attendants]

MACBETH	Bring me no more reports; let them fly all:
	Till Birnam wood remove to Dunsinane
	I cannot taint with fear. What's the boy Malcolm?
	Was he not born of woman? The spirits that know
	All mortal consequences have pronounc'd me thus:
	'Fear not, Macbeth; no man that's born of woman
	Shall e'er have power upon thee.' Then fly, false thanes,
	And mingle with the English epicures:
	The mind I sway by and the heart I bear
	Shall never sag with doubt nor shake with fear.
	[Enter a Servant]
	The devil damn thee black, thou cream-fac'd loon!
	Where gott'st thou that goose look?

SERVANT There is ten thousand—

MACBETH   Geese, villain?

SERVANT   Soldiers, sir.

MACBETH	Go, prick thy face, and over-red thy fear,
	Thou lily-liver'd boy. What soldiers, patch?
	Death of thy soul! those linen checks of thine
	Are counsellors to fear. What soldiers, whey-face?

SERVANT The English force, so please you.

MACBETH	Take thy face hence. *[Exit Servant]*
	Seyton!—I am sick at heart
	When I behold—Seyton, I say!—This push
	Will cheer me ever or disseat me now.
	I have liv'd long enough: my way of life
	Is fall'n into the sear, the yellow leaf;
	And that which should accompany old age,
	As honour, love, obedience, troops of friends,
	I must not look to have; but, in their stead,
	Curses, not loud but deep, mouth-honour, breath,
	Which the poor heart would fain deny, and dare not.
	Seyton!
	[Enter SEYTON]

SEYTON What is your gracious pleasure?

ORIGINAL

ACT V, SCENE 3

Dunsinane. A room in the castle.

[Enter MACBETH, Doctor, and Attendants]

MACBETH   Don't bother reporting desertions. Let them run away.
I have no reason to fear until Birnam wood attacks
Dunsinane castle.What is Malcolm? Isn't he a normal
human being? The witches that know all human fate
have prophesied that no one born of woman shall over-
power Macbeth. Then let the deserting lords escape and
join the English softies. My heart and mind shall have no
fear of them. *[Enter a Servant]* May Satan turn you black,
you white-faced fool! What makes you quiver like a goose?

SERVANT   There are ten thousand—

MACBETH   Geese, you turncoat?

SERVANT   Enemy soldiers, sir.

MACBETH   Go and pinch your cheeks to put color on your scared
face, you lily-livered boy. What soldiers are coming,
clown? May your soul rot! Your linen-white face scares
others. What soldiers are coming, milk-cheeks?

SERVANT   The English army, sir.

MACBETH   Take your face out of my sight. *[Exit Servant]* Seyton!—
I am sick at heart when I see—Seyton, I'm calling you!—
this revolt, which will either please me or end my reign.
I have lived a full life; my behavior has withered like a
yellowing leaf. I will never have the common rewards of
old age—honor, love, obedience, friends. Instead, I am
silently, deeply despised. Men honor me only with words.
They would like to deny their allegiance, but they are
afraid of me. Seyton! *[Enter SEYTON]*

SEYTON   What can I do for you?

MACBETH	What news more?	30
SEYTON	All is confirm'd, my Lord, which was reported.	
MACBETH	I'll fight till from my bones my flesh be hack'd. Give me my armour.	
SEYTON	'Tis not needed yet.	
MACBETH	I'll put it on. Send out more horses, skirr the country round; Hang those that talk of fear. Give me mine armour. How does your patient, doctor?	35
DOCTOR	Not so sick, my lord, As she is troubled with thick-coming fancies, That keep her from her rest.	
MACBETH	Cure her of that: Canst thou not minister to a mind diseas'd, Pluck from the memory a rooted sorrow, Raze out the written troubles of the brain, And with some sweet oblivious antidote Cleanse the stuff'd bosom of that perilous stuff Which weighs upon the heart?	40
DOCTOR	Therein the patient Must minister to himself.	45
MACBETH	Throw physic to the dogs; I'll none of it. Come, put mine armour on; give me my staff. Seyton, send out.—Doctor, the thanes fly from me.— Come sir dispatch.—If thou could'st doctor cast The water of my land, find her disease, And purge it to a sound and pristine health, I would applaud thee to the very echo, That should applaud again.—Pull't off, I say.— What rhubarb, senna, or what purgative drug Would scour these English hence? Hear'st thou of them?	50 55
DOCTOR	Ay, my good Lord; your royal preparation Makes us hear something.	
MACBETH	Bring it after me. I will not be afraid of death and bane Till Birnam forest come to Dunsinane.	60
DOCTOR	*[Aside]* Were I from Dunsinane away and clear, Profit again should hardly draw me here. *[Exeunt]*	

ORIGINAL

MACBETH	Is there any more news?
SEYTON	We have confirmed the earlier reports, my lord.
MACBETH	I will fight until the enemy hacks the meat from my bones. Give me my armor.
SEYTON	It is too soon for armor.
MACBETH	I want to put on my armor. Send out cavalry to scour the country. Hang citizens who say they are afraid. Give me my armor. How is Lady Macbeth, doctor?
DOCTOR	Not physically ill, my lord. She is mentally tormented by overwhelming illusions that give her no rest.
MACBETH	Heal her of her imaginings. Can't you cure mental illness, rid her mind of sorrow, erase troubles, and purify a suffering heart with a sedative?
DOCTOR	For that illness, the patient must heal himself.
MACBETH	Come, buckle my armor on me. Hand me my royal staff. Seyton, send out soldiers. Doctor, the lords desert me— Come, Seyton, hurry. Doctor, if you could diagnose Scotland's disease and wipe it out, I would glorify you for restoring the country to its former health. Remove my armor, I say.—What cleansing herb—rhubarb or senna— would wipe away these English troops? Have you heard of their approach?
DOCTOR	Yes, my lord. We heard your army's preparation for battle.
MACBETH	Bring my armor and follow me. I will not fear death or harm until Birnam forest attacks Dunsinane.
DOCTOR	*[Speaking to himself]* If I were safely away from Dunsinane castle, I would never return just to earn a medical fee. *[They depart]*

ACT V

TRANSLATION

ACT V, SCENE 4

Country near Birnam Wood.

[Enter, with drum and colours, MALCOLM, OLD SIWARD and his Son, MACDUFF, MENTEITH, CAITHNESS, ANGUS, LENNOX, ROSS, and Soldiers marching]

MALCOLM   Cousins, I hope the days are near at hand
That chambers will be safe.

MENTEITH   We doubt it nothing.

SIWARD   What wood is this before us?

MENTEITH   The wood of Birnam.

MALCOLM   Let every soldier hew him down a bough
And bear 't before him: thereby shall we shadow   5
The numbers of our host, and make discovery
Err in report of us.

SOLDIERS   It shall be done.

SIWARD   We learn no other but the confident tyrant
Keeps still in Dunsinane, and will endure
Our setting down before 't.

MALCOLM   'Tis his main hope;   10
For where there is advantage to be given,
Both more and less have given him the revolt,
And none serve with him but constrained things
Whose hearts are absent too.

MACDUFF   Let our just censures
Attend the true event, and put we on   15
Industrious soldiership.

SIWARD   The time approaches
That will with due decision make us know
What we shall say we have and what we owe.
Thoughts speculative, their unsure hopes relate,
But certain issue strokes must arbitrate,   20
Towards which advance the war.
[Exeunt, marching]

ORIGINAL

ACT V, SCENE 4

Country near Birnam Wood.

[MALCOLM, SIWARD THE ELDER and his Son, MACDUFF, MENTEITH, CAITHNESS, ANGUS, LENNOX, ROSS, and troops march in with drummer and flag bearers]

MALCOLM	Kinsmen, I hope that the time is near when homes will be safe.
MENTEITH	We have no doubt.
SIWARD	What forest is this ahead?
MENTEITH	It is Birnam wood.
MALCOLM	Let each soldier cut a branch to carry in front of him. With camouflage, we can conceal the number of our forces and encourage false estimates of rebel troop strength to Macbeth's army.
SOLDIERS	We will do what you ask.
SIWARD	We have learned that Macbeth is holed up in Dunsinane castle. He is confident and will wait out our arrival at the front gate.
MALCOLM	It's his only hope. Although he could claim more forces for his side, Scots of all classes have deserted him. The only people who remain on his side have no choice but to obey.
MACDUFF	Let our just claim against Macbeth accompany our attack. Let us display vigorous military strength.
SIWARD	The time is coming that will prove whether we will win or not. The proof of our speculation lies in the blows we inflict with our weapons in battle. *[They march out]*

TRANSLATION

ACT V, SCENE 5

Dunsinane. Within the castle.

[Enter, with a drum and colours, MACBETH, SEYTON, and Soldiers]

MACBETH   Hang out our banners on the outward walls;
The cry is still, 'They come;' our castle's strength
Will laugh a siege to scorn; here let them lie
Till famine and the ague eat them up;
Were they not forc'd with those that should be ours,   5
We might have met them dareful, beard to beard,
And beat them backward home.
                                    [A cry of women within]
                                    What is that noise?

SEYTON   It is the cry of women, my good lord. *[Exit]*

MACBETH   I have almost forgot the taste of fears.
The time has been my senses would have cool'd   10
To hear a night-shriek, and my fell of hair
Would at a dismal treatise rouse and stir
As life were in 't. I have supp'd full with horrors;
Direness, familiar to my slaughterous thoughts,
Cannot once start me.
                                    [Re-enter SEYTON]
                                    Wherefore was that cry?   15

SEYTON   The queen, my Lord, is dead.

MACBETH   She should have died hereafter;
There would have been a time for such a word.
To-morrow, and to-morrow, and to-morrow,
Creeps in this petty pace from day to day,   20
To the last syllable of recorded time;
And all our yesterdays have lighted fools
The way to dusty death. Out, out, brief candle!
Life's but a walking shadow, a poor player
That struts and frets his hour upon the stage,   25
And then is heard no more; it is a tale
Told by an idiot, full of sound and fury,
Signifying nothing.
                                    [Enter a Messenger]
                                    Thou com'st to use thy tongue; thy story quickly.

MESSENGER   Gracious my Lord,   30
I should report that which I say I saw,
But know not how to do it.

ORIGINAL

ACT V, SCENE 5

Dunsinane. Within the castle.

[MACBETH, SEYTON, and soldiers enter with a drummer and flag bearers]

MACBETH   Suspend our flags on the outside of the walls. The English continue marching toward us. This castle is strong enough to outlast their attack. Let them camp here till they die of hunger and fever. If Malcolm and Macduff had not forced disloyal Scots to rebel, we could have confronted the English man to man and repelled them from Scotland. *[A cry of women within]* What is that outcry?

SEYTON   It is women wailing, my lord. *[He goes out]*

MACBETH   I had almost forgotten terror. There was a time I would have shivered to hear cries in the night and my hair would have stood on end as though it had a life of its own. I have swallowed my share of horror. Now, terror is so familiar to my murderous thoughts that I am no longer startled. *[Re-enter SEYTON]* Where did the cry come from?

SEYTON   My lord, the queen has died.

MACBETH   She would have died soon anyway. She would have met death in the usual way. Days pass by monotonously just as they have from the beginning of time. All past history has seen the lives and deaths of fools. Gone, gone, short life! We are shadow figures who cross the stage, acting out our parts, and then falling silent. Life is a senseless tale filled with meaningless emotion. *[Enter a Messenger]* You have a message for me. Out with it.

MESSENGER   My lord, I have disturbing news I can't put into words.

ACT V

TRANSLATION

MACBETH   Well, say, sir.

MESSENGER   As I did stand my watch upon the hill,
I look'd towards Birnam, and anon, methought,
The wood began to move.

MACBETH   Liar and slave!   35

MESSENGER   Let me endure your wrath if 't be not so;
Within this three mile you may see it coming;
I say, a moving grove.

MACBETH   If thou speak'st false,
Upon the next tree shalt thou hang alive,
Till famine cling thee; if thy speech be sooth,   40
I care not if thou dost for me as much.
I pull in resolution and begin
To doubt the equivocation of the fiend
That lies like truth; 'Fear not, till Birnam wood
Do come to Dunsinane;' and now a wood   45
Comes toward Dunsinane. Arm, arm, and out!
If this which he avouches does appear,
There is nor flying hence, nor tarrying here.
I 'gin to be aweary of the sun,
And wish the estate o' the world were now undone.   50
Ring the alarum-bell! Blow, wind! come, wrack!
At least we'll die with harness on our back.
[Exeunt]

MACBETH	Say it, man.
MESSENGER	While I was standing guard on the hill, I thought I saw Birnam wood moving.
MACBETH	Liar! Scum!
MESSENGER	I will suffer your punishment if I am lying. From three miles away, you can see the grove in motion.
MACBETH	If you are lying, you will hang on a tree until you starve. If you are telling the truth, I don't care if you execute me in the same way. My determination is shaken. I doubt the devil's own truth. "Don't be afraid until Birnam wood comes to Dunsinane" and now the forest is approaching Dunsinane castle. Soldiers to arms and move out! If the messenger's words come true, there is no safety either in running away or in remaining here. I am tired of living and wish that the world would fall to ruin. Ring the alarm bell! Let the wind blow and destruction advance. At least we will die in armor. *[They go out]*

ACT V, SCENE 6

The same. A plain before the castle.

*[Enter, with drum and colours, MALCOLM, OLD SIWARD, MACDUFF, etc.,
and their Army, with boughs]*

MALCOLM
Now near enough; your leavy screens throw down,
And show like those you are. You, worthy uncle,
Shall, with my cousin, your right-noble son,
Lead our first battle; worthy Macduff and we
Shall take upon's what else remains to do,   5
According to our order.

SIWARD
                                                    Fare you well.
Do we but find the tyrant's power to-night,
Let us be beaten, if we cannot fight.

MACDUFF
Make all our trumpets speak; give them all breath,
Those clamorous harbingers of blood and death.   10
[Exeunt]

ACT V, SCENE 6

The same. A plain before the castle.

*[MALCOLM, SIWARD THE ELDER, MACDUFF, etc., and their troops, camou-
flaged with tree branches, march with drummer and flag bearers]*

MALCOLM   We are in position. Toss down your branches and reveal
yourselves to Macbeth.Uncle Siward, you and your noble
son, Siward the Younger, will lead the attack. Macduff
and I will follow and complete the assault as we have
planned.

SIWARD   Farewell. If we engage Macbeth's troops tonight, we
ought to lose the battle if we don't fight them off.

MACDUFF   Sound all the trumpets. Turn them into messengers of
blood and death. *[They go out]*

ACT V, SCENE 7

The same. Another part of the plain.

[Alarums. Enter MACBETH]

MACBETH   They have tied me to a stake; I cannot fly,
But bear-like I must fight the course. What's he
That was not born of woman? Such a one
Am I to fear, or none.
[Enter YOUNG SIWARD]

YOUNG SIWARD What is thy name?

MACBETH   Thou'lt be afraid to hear it.   5

YOUNG SIWARD No; though thou call'st thyself a hotter name
Than any is in hell.

MACBETH   My name's Macbeth.

YOUNG SIWARD The devil himself could not pronounce a title
More hateful to mine ear.

MACBETH   No, nor more fearful.

YOUNG SIWARD Thou liest, abhorred tyrant; with my sword   10
I'll prove the lie thou speak'st.
[They fight and YOUNG SIWARD is slain]

MACBETH   Thou wast born of woman:
But swords I smile at, weapons laugh to scorn,
Brandish'd by man that's of a woman born. *[Exit]*
[Alarums. Enter MACDUFF]

MACDUFF   That way the noise is. Tyrant, show thy face:
If thou be'st slain and with no stroke of mine,   15
My wife and children's ghosts will haunt me still.
I cannot strike at wretched kerns, whose arms
Are hir'd to bear their staves: either thou, Macbeth,
Or else my sword with an unbatter'd edge
I sheathe again undeeded. There thou should'st be;   20
By this great clatter, one of greatest note
Seems bruited. Let me find him, fortune!
And more I beg not. *[Exit. Alarums]*
[Enter MALCOLM and OLD SIWARD]

ORIGINAL

ACT V, SCENE 7

Before Macbeth's castle on another part of the field.

[Alarms sound. MACBETH enters]

MACBETH   They have tied me to a post like a bear facing wild dogs. I can't escape. I must fight as best I can. Where is the man who had an abnormal birth? He is the only soldier I fear. *[Enter SIWARD THE YOUNGER]*

YOUNG SIWARD Who are you?

MACBETH   My name will terrorize you.

YOUNG SIWARD No. You can't frighten me, even if your name is Satan.

MACBETH   I am Macbeth.

YOUNG SIWARD You are a more hateful enemy than Satan himself.

MACBETH   No, nor more fearful. Satan is no more terrible than I.

YOUNG SIWARD You are a liar, hated tyrant. I will prove you false with my sword. *[They fight and SIWARD THE YOUNGER is slain]*

MACBETH   You are a normal man. I scoff at your sword and scorn other weapons when ordinary warriors wield them. *[Exit]* *[Alarms sound. Enter MACDUFF]*

MACDUFF   I hear the sound of a duel. Tyrant, come out of hiding. If some other soldier kills you, the spirits of my wife and children will continue to haunt me. I can't waste my energies fighting ordinary soldiers whom you have hired to bear arms. Either I kill you, Macbeth, or else I sheathe my sword without striking a blow. You should be somewhere close. I hear sounds of fighting. Lady luck, let me find him and I will ask for nothing more. *[Exit. Alarm sounds]* *[Enter MALCOLM and SIWARD THE ELDER]*

ACT V

TRANSLATION

SIWARD   This way, my lord; the castle's gently render'd:
The tyrant's people on both sides do fight;   25
The noble thanes do bravely in the war;
The day almost itself professes yours,
And little is to do.

MALCOLM   We have met with foes
That strike beside us.

SIWARD   Enter, sir, the castle. *[Exeunt. Alarums]*

SIWARD	This way, Malcolm. Macbeth has given up the castle without a fight. Scots join both sides of the rebellion. Scottish lords fight splendidly in war. You have won a victory. There isn't much left to do.
MALCOLM	We have encountered enemy troops that deliberately tried to miss hitting us.
SIWARD	Enter the castle, sir. *[They depart. Alarms sound]*

ACT V

ACT V, SCENE 8

The same. Another part of the plain.

[Re-enter MACBETH]

MACBETH   Why should I play the Roman fool, and die
On mine own sword? whiles I see lives, the gashes
Do better upon them.
[Re-enter MACDUFF]

MACDUFF   Turn, hell-hound, turn!

MACBETH   Of all men else I have avoided thee:
But get thee back, my soul is too much charg'd   5
With blood of thine already.

MACDUFF   I have no words;
My voice is in my sword, thou bloodier villain
Than terms can give thee out! *[They fight]*

MACBETH   Thou losest labour:
As easy mayst thou the intrenchant air
With thy keen sword impress as make me bleed: 10
Let fall thy blade on vulnerable crests;
I bear a charmed life, which must not yield
To one of woman born.

MACDUFF   Despair thy charm;
And let the angel whom thou still hast serv'd
Tell thee, Macduff was from his mother's womb   15
Untimely ripp'd.

MACBETH   Accursed be that tongue that tells me so,
For it hath cow'd my better part of man:
And be these juggling fiends no more believ'd,
That palter with us in a double sense;   20
That keep the word of promise to our ear,
And break it to our hope. I'll not fight with thee.

MACDUFF   Then yield thee, coward,
And live to be the show and gaze o' the time:
We'll have thee, as our rarer monsters are,   25
Painted upon a pole, and underwrit,
'Here may you see the tyrant.'

ORIGINAL

ACT V, SCENE 8

Before Macbeth's castle on another part of the field.

[Re-enter MACBETH]

MACBETH	Why should I die like a suicidal Roman by falling on my own sword? While I see enemy soldiers still alive, the wounds look better on them than on me. *[Re-enter MACDUFF]*
MACDUFF	Face me, hell-hound!
MACBETH	Of all the enemy soldiers, I have tried to avoid you. Go away. My conscience already carries the sin of murdering your family.
MACDUFF	I have nothing to say to you. I will let my sword speak for me. You are a more vicious killer than words can describe. *[They fight]*
MACBETH	You waste your energy. Thrusting your sharp sword at my flesh is as useless as fighting air. Aim your blade at more vulnerable men. I am fated to yield only to a man not born of woman.
MACDUFF	Abandon your magic. Let the demon you serve inform you that Macduff was not born normally. He was cut from his mother's womb.
MACBETH	I curse your tongue for telling me. You have slain my courage. Let no one believe prophets that bandy words and give them double meanings. They whisper promises in our ears and destroy our hopes. I won't fight back.
MACDUFF	Then surrender, coward, and survive as an exhibit. We will put you on display to be gawked at. We will paint your picture on a pole like a freak and add the caption, "You may view the tyrant here."

TRANSLATION

MACBETH   I will not yield,
To kiss the ground before young Malcolm's feet,
And to be baited with the rabble's curse.
Though Birnam wood be come to Dunsinane,   30
And thou oppos'd, being of no woman born,
Yet I will try the last: before my body
I throw my war-like shield. Lay on, Macduff,
And damn'd be him that first cries, 'Hold, enough!'
[Exeunt, fighting]
[Retreat. Flourish. Reenter, with drum and colours,
MALCOLM, OLD SIWARD, ROSS, Thanes, and Soldiers]

MALCOLM   I would the friends we miss were safe arriv'd.   35

SIWARD   Some must go off: and yet, by these I see,
So great a day as this is cheaply bought.

MALCOLM   Macduff is missing, and your noble son.

ROSS   Your son, my lord, has paid a soldier's debt:
He only liv'd but till he was a man;   40
The which no sooner had his prowess confirm'd
In the unshrinking station where he fought,
But like a man he died.

SIWARD   Then he is dead?

ROSS   Ay, and brought off the field. Your cause of sorrow
Must not be measur'd by his worth, for then   45
It hath no end.

SIWARD   Had he his hurts before?

ROSS   Ay, on the front.

SIWARD   Why then, God's soldier be he!
Had I as many sons as I have hairs,
I would not wish them to a fairer death:
And so, his knell is knoll'd.

MALCOLM   He's worth more sorrow,   50
And that I'll spend for him.

SIWARD   He's worth no more;
They say he parted well, and paid his score:
And so, God be with him! Here comes newer comfort.
[Re-enter MACDUFF, with MACBETH's head]

MACBETH	I won't surrender and grovel before Malcolm. I won't be exhibited before Scottish peasants. Even if Birnam wood comes to Dunsinane castle and even if you were not born of woman, I will fight to the end. I toss my war shield in front of me. Come at me, Macduff, and damnation to the man who first gives up the fight. *[They go out still fighting] [Macbeth's army sounds retreat. A bustle announces the return of MALCOLM, SIWARD THE ELDER, ROSS, lords, and soldiers with a drummer and flag bearers]*
MALCOLM	I wish that all my supporters had survived the battle.
SIWARD	War always kills. We have lost few soldiers in winning so great a victory.
MALCOLM	We are missing Macduff and Siward the Younger.
ROSS	Your son, Siward, has died like a soldier. He lived only to young manhood. After showing his skill in battle and in facing the enemy without fear, he died like a man.
SIWARD	Are you sure he is dead?
ROSS	Yes. His body has been recovered from the battlefield. If you grieve for him as he deserves, you will never end your sorrow.
SIWARD	Did he die of wounds to the front of his body?
ROSS	Yes. On the front.
SIWARD	Then he was a holy warrior. If I had as many sons as I have hairs, I would not wish them a more honorable death. So, Siward the Younger has perished.
MALCOLM	He deserves our grief. I will honor him with my sorrow.
SIWARD	He is worth no more than you can give him. He died well and paid his debts. May God receive him! Here comes better news. *[Re-enter MACDUFF, with MACBETH's head]*

ACT V

TRANSLATION

MACDUFF   Hail, king, for so thou art. Behold, where stands
                The usurper's cursed head: the time is free: 55
                I see thee compass'd with thy kingdom's pearl,
                That speak my salutation in their minds;
                Whose voices I desire aloud with mine;
                Hail, King of Scotland!

ALL   Hail, King of Scotland! *[Flourish]*

MALCOLM   We shall not spend a large expense of time   60
                Before we reckon with your several loves,
                And make us even with you. My thanes and kinsmen,
                Henceforth be earls, the first that ever Scotland
                In such an honour nam'd. What's more to do,
                Which would be planted newly with the time,   65
                As calling home our exil'd friends abroad
                That fled the snares of watchful tyranny;
                Producing forth the cruel ministers
                Of this dead butcher and his fiend-like queen,
                Who, as 'tis thought, by self and violent hands   70
                Took off her life; this, and what needful else
                That calls upon us, by the grace of Grace
                We will perform in measure, time, and place:
                So, thanks to all at once and to each one,
                Whom we invite to see us crown'd at Scone.   75
                [Flourish. Exeunt]

MACDUFF   Hail, King Malcolm, for that is your new title. See, I
carry Macbeth's cursed head. Scotland is free. I see
you surrounded with the best of Scotland's soldiers.
They are already thinking that you are their king.
I urge them to shout with me, "Hail, King of Scotland!"

ALL   Hail, King of Scotland! *[A stir among the soldiers]*

MALCOLM   Shortly, I will estimate how well you have served me and
repay you for your loyalty. My lords and kinsmen, I grant
you the title of earls, the first in Scotland's history. I have
other duties to perform in the future. I want to summon
home Scots who fled Macbeth's spying and tyranny.
Assassins worked for this butchering king and his fiendish
wife, who may have committed suicide. This and other
tasks, with God's help, I will finish at the appropriate time
and place. I thank each member of our troops, whom
I invite to witness my crowning at Scone, Scotland's
traditional coronation site. *[Crowd noise. All depart]*

ACT V

TRANSLATION

Questions for Reflection

1. What does Lady Macbeth learn about crime? Examine the multiple ironies of Lady Macbeth's sleepwalking and suicide. Compare her need of a candle and her compulsive handwashing to the events surrounding Duncan's murder. Consider why Shakespeare depicts her as overconfident.

2. How does Macbeth redeem himself by refusing to run from Macduff? Compare the execution of the first Thane of Cawdor in Act I with Macbeth's last moments in Act V.

3. In what way do Macbeth, Siward the Younger, and the first Thane of Cawdor die honorably? How does Macduff's son display a similar honor?

4. Why is the loss of an heir significant to Macbeth? to Malcolm? to Scotland? to King Edward? to Macduff? Look for lines from the play that suggest that Macbeth and his wife had at least one child, who didn't survive.

5. How does Banquo reveal a worthier character than his companion? When does he suspect that Macbeth has a different attitude toward prophecy? Contrast Macbeth's and Banquo's reactions to the witches' first predictions.

6. Consider the deaths of two sons and the near execution of another in the play. Why does Shakespeare stress the parent/child relationship? What does he suggest about Duncan's regard for Malcolm as heir apparent. Explain how the loss of children gives Macduff courage.

7. Why do the Scots choose silence, suspicion, rumors, feigned loyalty, and exile rather than accuse Macbeth directly of murder and corruption. Consider how the uncertain loyalty of Scots impacts Act V. Explain why Shakespeare stresses Macbeth's successive demands that someone bring his armor and why he abandons his shield during the final duel with Macduff.

8. What forms of prejudice do the witches reveal in their spell? Why would English playgoers understand bigotry toward Turks, Jews, Tartars, witches, prostitutes, and illegitimate babies?

9. What are the causes and symptoms of depression that Shakespeare presents in the play? How does a guilty conscience contribute to Macbeth's hallucinations? Why does the doctor suspect that Lady Macbeth may try to kill herself?

10. What strengths do Edward, Malcolm, Macduff, Siward the Elder, and Siward the Younger contribute to the ten thousand English soldiers? Consider why camouflage is a useful ploy in wartime. Also, why might a long siege at Dunsinane castle promote famine and fever and defeat the rebels? Why does Dunsinane crumble from within?

11. How does King Edward set a worthy example for Malcolm, the crown prince of Scotland? What Christ-like qualities are evident in Edward? How do the laying on of hands and the blessing of sick peasants reward England's king and his subjects? How does his reward system compare with that of Duncan? of Macbeth? of Malcolm?

12. Why does Macbeth conceal from his wife a plan to ambush and assassinate Banquo and Fleance? Consider why Shakespeare depicts Macbeth as excessively cruel. Also consider why a third murderer helps ambush Banquo and Fleance. Is Macbeth's spy system effective?

13. Account for Macbeth's shame at meeting Macduff in Act V. Why does the murder of Macduff's family seem more evil and less excusable than the murders of Duncan and Banquo, the false accusations of Donalbain and Malcolm, and the attack on Fleance? In what way does Macduff "dispute it like a man"?

14. How does Shakespeare incorporate into the play the highlights of Scottish history up to the crowning of James VI of Scotland as James I of England? What does Macbeth see in the mirror? What more does he want to learn from the illusions?

15. What do you predict the strengths of Malcolm's reign will be? Consider Malcolm's relationship with King Edward, Macduff, and Siward the Elder, and with Donalbain, who chooses not to join the rebel army. Why would the son of a murdered king be especially cautious of his enemies and generous to his supporters, the new earls of Scotland?

16. How does Macbeth's reign compare to those of other evil rulers of history? What sets him on a downhill course toward deceiving, manipulating, spying, killing, and hiring mercenaries to protect him? Why does Macbeth seem weary of his own crimes? Why is he ready to die?

17. How do the leadership qualities in Macbeth, Hecate, Lady Macbeth, Macduff, Edward, Duncan, Donalbain, Banquo, Siward the Elder, Macduff's son, and Malcolm compare to each other? Note the qualities that they share or lack. Why does Donalbain seem younger and less experienced than his brother?

18. Why is the murder of Duncan a breach of an age-old custom of in-house hospitality? Why is Lady Macbeth's fainting spell believable? Consider the ancient Greek prohibition against guests harming hosts and hosts harming guests.

19. How does Shakespeare present the theme of illusion versus reality in the play? How do Hecate and the witches lead Macbeth toward self-destruction? Why does he see a floating dagger and the ghost of Banquo? Why is the duel with Macduff the end of Macbeth's illusion and the beginning of his confrontation with reality? How does the beheading of his corpse illustrate the reality of punishment for a criminal?

20. How would you justify the battlefield promotion of the Thane of Glamis to the Thane of Cawdor? Consider why Duncan chooses a combat setting rather than a post-war ritual.

21. How would you compose an extended definition of reverse psychology by using as an example Malcolm's claim to be lustful and greedy? How does this deception test Macduff's sincerity? Why does Malcolm need to test the loyalty of other Scots? Why does he depend on second-hand reports?

22. What is the tone of the "tomorrow and tomorrow" speech? Consider why Macbeth compares himself to an actor playing a part, and also how Shakespeare creates irony out of a speech that has become one of the most re-enacted of all English drama.

23. How does Macduff channel grief into military might? Why does he insist on killing Macbeth with his own sword? How does the beheading of Scotland's tyrant king both violate and uphold the concept of divine right of kings?

24. How would you define comic relief using examples from the porter's speech at the gate of Macbeth's castle? Why does Shakespeare picture the porter imagining that he guards the gate to hell?

25. Why are Duncan's sons wise to flee from Macbeth's castle before a thorough investigation of Duncan's murder? How does Macbeth cast doubt on his version of the murder?

26. How does Shakespeare use perversions of nature to account for the slaying of a good king and the rise of a tyrant king? Consider why the witches choose animal parts, wind, thunder, the moon, storms, and waves as means of tormenting humans. Also, why does the witch compare the "pricking of my thumbs" with the approach of Macbeth?

27. What are some of the bird images in the play? What does the "night bird" symbolize? In what way is Lady Macduff a hen guarding her chicks? Why does the building of a martin nest at Inverness castle create a false image of comfort and safety? In what way does Macbeth become a "hell-kite"?

28. What does Shakespeare imply in Lady Macbeth's observation that Duncan's body contained much blood? How does the king's free-flowing blood typify the extremes of Macbeth's rule? Consider how the play justifies the Elizabethan belief that God sanctified rulers.

29. How does the last scene describe feudalism? What is Malcolm's system of rewards to loyal followers? Why is it advantageous for him to invite the rebels to his crowning at Scone?

30. Why does Lady Macbeth lie to her dinner guests that Macbeth has long suffered from delusions? What does her willingness to deceive suggest about her qualifications to be a hostess? to be Macbeth's wife? to be Scotland's queen?

31. How does Shakespeare use light and dark as symbols of goodness and evil? What do phases of the moon foreshadow about the action? What does Lady Macbeth's lighted taper suggest about her guilty conscience? Why does Banquo need a light during his ride with Fleance?

32. How does Shakespeare justify revolution? How could his somber drama jeopardize his standing with England's ruler? How did strife affect the reign of Queen Elizabeth I and the succession of James I? In what ways are Queen Elizabeth I and Macbeth in similar situations regarding an heir to the throne?

33. Why do the witches identify Macbeth as "something wicked"? How has Macbeth changed since his first encounter with the witches. Does Shakespeare exonerate Hecate and the witches for unleashing Macbeth's penchant for murder?

34. Does the conniving of the witches, Hecate, and Lady Macbeth indicate Shakespeare's distrust of women? Why does Macduff's son suspect his mother would escape widowhood into a quick and easy second marriage? How does Macduff honor Duncan's wife?

35. How would you defend Lady Macduff's accusation that her husband abandoned her and his helpless children? What choices did he have? What action might have been less painful, less catastrophic than his fleeing to England? Consider how his choices rob him of an heir to Fife castle.

36. How do Macbeth and Lady Macbeth complement each other's strengths and weaknesses? Why do their deaths seem justified? Why does the play not clarify how Lady Macbeth died?

37. How does the gift of a diamond symbolize Lady Macbeth's hard, cold exterior and her stony heart?

38. How does Shakespeare use lowly people in a drama about kings, queens, princes, and lords? How do cast members like the porter, the white-faced servant, messengers, Lady Macduff's servants, Seyton, Lady Macbeth's lady-in-waiting, and Duncan's grooms contribute to the action?

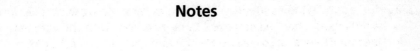

Notes

Notes

Notes

Notes

Notes

No more "Double, double, toil and trouble…"
You can learn Shakespeare on the Double!™

Shakespeare on the Double!™ books make understanding the Bard as easy and painless as this one does. The most comprehensive guides available, they include an easy-to-understand translation alongside the original text, *plus:*

- A brief synopsis of the basic plot and action that provides a broad understanding of the play
- A character list with an in-depth description of the characteristics, motivations, and actions of each major player
- A visual character map that identifies the major characters and how they relate to one another
- A cycle-of-death graphic that pinpoints the sequence of deaths in the play, including who dies, how they die, and why
- Reflective questions that help you identify and delve deeper into the themes and meanings of the play

All *Shakespeare on the Double!* Books
$8.99 US/$10.99 CAN/£5.99 UK • 5¹/₂ x 8¹/₂ • 192–264 pages

The next time you delve into the Bard's masterpieces, get help—on the double!

Available wherever books are sold.

WILEY
Now you know.